LOVE IS SALTY

IT'S DEFINITELY HATE!

NICKI GRACE

For anyone who has experienced the roller coaster of love I hope you found your happiness, and if not, I'm sure it's on the way.

CHAPTER 1

Piper pulled the trigger, and Scott's body fell to the ground. She smirked as the smell of gun powder filled her nose and thin lines of smoke rose from the barrel. That bastard had just gotten what he deserved.

"See, didn't that feel good?" Lish asked, patting her on the back.

Piper lowered the gun.

"It did."

"I told you. All you had to do was imagine it was Scott. Now you've released some steam and avoided jail time."

The cardboard cut-out popped back up, ready for more punishment and sporting several holes that could be fatal if he were alive.

"You are a wise woman, Lish. That fucking asshole. Lying to me all this time. Who the hell does that?"

Piper was reloading the gun and trying to keep her thoughts in order. She had been to the range a few times before for fun and to learn how to handle a gun, but today, it was different; today was revenge-driven. She wanted to strangle Scott. The depths he had gone to lie to her and his wife were inexcusable, shocking, and sociopathic.

"Sadly, people lie and deceive others much too often. I knew something was off about him, but I didn't expect this. I thought maybe he liked to wear women's underwear or run around naked in public."

"Please stop trying to make me laugh. I'm upset, and my stupidity is embarrassing. I'm such an idiot."

"It's you and me, Piper," she said in a voice meant to mimic Scott's and fired off a shot.

"I love you, Piper," she said and fired off another.

"Don't you trust me, baby?"

She sent a final bullet through the unlucky male image that was receiving the fate of another.

"They should allow you to upload sound in here. That way, I can add Scott's voice and feel like I'm giving him his due diligence."

Lish laughed.

"That may be a good idea; you should put it in the suggestion box. In the meantime, do you feel better?"

Piper lowered the gun and considered the question.

"I do. I still want to tie him to a sign and throw darts at him, but this was a fun way to blow off some steam."

"Anytime, bestie. You ready for lunch?"

"I am if you're in the mood for tacos."

"At The Taco Hole?"

"Yes."

"I'm in the mood then."

Piper fired one last round into the target and prepared to leave.

They arrived at the Taco Hole and were escorted to a small booth-style table by the window. The place wasn't huge but served some of the best tacos Piper had ever tasted. For a few minutes, they were quiet. Lish was checking her phone while Piper enjoyed the music coming from the speakers and watching others socialize. Everyone looked so happy and full of life, while she only felt varying levels of indignation.

Not just at Scott but also at herself and at the law for making murder illegal. She sank into her seat, and Lish gave her a sympathetic smile.

"Want some ice cream too?" Lish asked.

"You're sweet. No, I'm fine. I can't believe Scott hid his wife and has been living a whole double, no correction, triple life right under my nose."

"Triple?"

Piper held up three fingers and wiggled each one to represent a different name.

"His wife, Simone and Me."

"Hmm, I guess that's true. So, Simone is stalker, crazy chick's name?"

Piper looked defeated again.

"I don't know. She never told me, and Scott always called her Simone, the nanny, which is evidently not true."

"What about Jasmine?"

"Dammit, that makes four women he's been lying to. How does he even keep up with all this?"

Lish made a face.

"What do you want to say, Lish?"

"Nothing!"

"Go ahead. I won't get mad. All my anger is on reserve for Scott."

"If I had to guess, I'd assume he got away with this by spending one week with each of you."

"Oh yeah, the 'I can only see you the week I'm off' excuse. It's not like I never contemplated that those long absences allotted him the chance to cheat. I just . . ."

"You rationalized it," Lish filled in, concluding Piper's thought.

"Pretty much. I've heard of men working in other states before to take care of their families. Haven't you?"

"True, but they are probably cheaters too."

Piper looked out the window, but more to have something to do rather than take in the scene. A memory occurred to her. One of Scott showing her a video of Ryan learning to walk. That meant the scrubs and clogs of the woman holding the camera belonged to his wife. Julia was in the picture all along. How had Scott been so heartless?

"He was so wonderful in the beginning," Piper said.

"They are all good in the beginning, and I think that's in the manual."

"Asshole!" Piper slammed a hand on the table.

It echoed a lot louder than intended and prompted a waitress to come over. She must have thought they were trying to get her attention.

"I'm so sorry. I'm the only one working the floor today. My name is Meg. What can I get you?"

Piper apologized for the noise and placed her order.

"I'll take five supreme tacos and a Sprite."

"I want the same except extra sour cream with mine," Lish added.

Meg jotted down their requests. Then she pocketed the pen and notepad, apologized again, and left to put in their order.

"What did his wife say after you told her you two are unintentionally sharing a man?"

"I think it broke her, Lish. She didn't say much of anything, just kinda stared off into space and nodded like it was a fate she suspected being married to him."

"That's it? I would have been flipping over your desk and giving Scott his walking papers."

"Julia's a nice lady, and I think she was in shock. Imagine if it were you who had met a stranger in the hallway at work. The next thing you know, you're being told she has been dating your husband for almost a year?"

"I would imagine that's when I slap her."

"Lish," Piper said, taking her friends' hands into her own. "Listen to me, no one got slapped."

Lish seemed slightly let down, and Piper laughed.

"Fine! No new juicy boxing stories," she said, rolling her eyes. "Continue your cordial and mature story. Did Julia only stare and agree with you the whole time?"

"At first, she told me I must be confused, but I told her I recognized her from the pictures in their home. I mean, it's hard to forget her face. Ryan looks so much like her. Anyway, then I provided her with proof using the images of Scott, me, and Ryan I had stored in my phone, and that was enough."

"You're right. I could not imagine being on the other end of that bombshell. How long have they been married?"

"About five years."

"Scott is a piece of shit. What did she say after you showed her the pictures?"

"Not a lot, she did make this sound that I can only describe as a wounded gasp and shook her head. I could see her whole world crumbling right before my eyes, and it was heartbreaking. I don't think she was surprised honestly. Hurt but not surprised."

"Yeah, women know when their men are liars. I think we just want to see the best in them no matter what."

"Exactly. She did say that things had felt off for a while with him, but there was always some excuse and no real-time to talk. Either he was busy, or she was, with work, taking care of Ryan, or get this, her sick mother."

"Wait. The grandparents that Scott claimed have been keeping Ryan?"

"The exact ones. They are in no position to take care of anyone. Julia's mom is bedridden, and her dad does all he can to take care of the mom. Julia has a full plate."

"Shit. No wonder Scott was living his life like a dog without a leash."

"Did you ask her what she is going to do?"

"No. We were at work, and I don't think either of us thought it appropriate to unpack our whole lives. But we plan to meet on Friday at my place to talk more in-depth."

"Is she going to say anything to Scott?"

"I didn't ask, but I doubt it. She strikes me as the type that wants the entire story first."

Lish sat back.

"Friday, huh?"

"Yup."

"Do you need me there in case she changes her mind and decides to beat your ass?"

"It might be best if you sit this one out. If Julia gets out of hand, I can handle myself."

"You are no fun."

"Besides, I have something to deal with."

"What's that?"

"Getting Jasmine to talk. She may be able to give us more insight on what Scott has been up to when he wasn't around the two of us."

"Any chance Jasmine is the girl behind the bloody pads, tire slashing and turning your number into a sex hotline?"

"The voice isn't the same and, I think the crazed girl is local. Jasmine is in Milwaukee."

Talking through all these details with Lish was stirring something dark in Piper. Scott could not get away with all of this. She'd spent a year letting this man touch her, pretend to love her and fuck her, in more ways than one, it seemed.

Without shame, he was receiving all the benefits with not enough doubt.

"Has Scott called?"

"Last we spoke we were not on good terms. Scott usually waits a few days when he is mad and then tries again with the charm and manipulation that has me questioning my sanity and dedication to our relationship."

"Ugh! The manipulation tactic, I've fallen victim to that more times than I'd like."

Piper shook her head as if doing so could make the horrible experiences vanish.

"Anyway, since Scott is out of the picture, what about Desmond?" Lish asked, lifting a brow.

"Nothing to report on that front, my friend. The last time I spoke to him was when he stopped by and Scott was there. I went by twice to speak to him and got no answer."

What she didn't say was that she missed him. Correction, she craved him. The naughty part of her thought about his dick a little more often than it should. How thick and long it was, how erotically good it felt in her mouth. Even the way he effortlessly slid into her body and sent her to places no man had before was her go-to material for daydreaming.

Her more vulnerable side longed for his company: the easy jokes, magnetic smile, and relaxed vibe. Somehow not seeing Desmond had made the issues with Scott harder to handle. Talking to him always made Piper feel powerful. She wished to tell him about her new job and how much she loved it, but lately, he'd been nowhere to be found.

Their server Meg came over and laid two trays of neatly stacked tacos in front of each of them. The steamy goodness put a smile on both girls' faces. Wasting no time, Piper picked up a taco, added tons of hot sauce, and took a bite.

The crunchy, tangy, spicy treat brought back memories of the first time she and Lish visited this restaurant. It was after they'd finished a shift at the Golden Bar. The evening had paid well, and they wanted to celebrate. Pulling into the parking lot of the first food place open, it was that night that, The Taco Hole became a new favorite of theirs.

The girls enjoyed a few more bites before resuming their conversation.

"Well, Lish, enough about my life. Besides public nudity, what else have you been up to?"

"A few dates here and there with no one special. Helping my sister take care of her three kids and, oh," she said, snapping her fingers together. "Ordering more cute clothes from your cousin's website."

"Yes! Fashion! Tell me more."

"I purchased four skirts, a half top, and two pairs of stylish lounge slippers. When are you going to be able to start shopping with me again? Spending excessive money alone makes me feel guilty. I need someone to blame."

"Very soon, I hope. I haven't received my first check. But after the money starts rolling in, I have to catch up on some bills, including paying you back for those tires." Lish tried to interrupt about the repayment, but Piper held up a hand. "Putting a little into savings, and then I'm free!" she said, stretching out the word and holding up a taco.

"Fantastic," Lish replied, taking another bit. "Are you doing anything for your birthday? It's in a few weeks."

"I will do what I do every year, nothing. You know my birthday doesn't matter to me. My mom wasn't around to make it special, and if she was, she forgot. It's just another day."

"I was hoping this year, you'd changed."

"Nope. But on my first free check. Let's do something fun."

"Like what?"

Piper thought about it.

"Want to get a sexy tattoo with me. You can show it off on stage and to your future love interests."

"On stage is a go, but a new love interest isn't happening. I haven't dated anyone I genuinely liked in a long time."

"Love strikes when you least expect it."

"Love and disaster," Lish stated, pointing a finger.

"I'm trying to be positive here."

"Right, right. Sorry. Hey, I have the perfect tattoo in mind."

"What?"

"A penis."

"Don't you get enough of those?" Piper asked.

"That's my point. I can get a picture of a penis tattooed on my inner thigh. That way, I can tell all the men just looking for a good time that my vaginal area is occupied, and they will leave me the hell alone."

Piper snickered, causing her hand to shake and some of her cheese and tomatoes fell off. Adding them back with another few splashes of hot sauce, she took another bite.

"What about the guys that want to be serious with you? You think they will like the idea of another dick being present?"

"Hmm. Obviously, I have not thought this through."

"Not at all," Piper agreed.

"It's a joke anyway. I'm simply tired of the drama with men. I want something serious, and I want to be happy. But judging from your love life, I better not hold my breath."

"Don't even try it. Do not use my problems as an excuse for you not finding love. Me getting trash does not mean you won't find treasure. You are an amazing woman with the world's biggest heart, a hot body, and you can throw your leg back further than any girl I know. You're a keeper Alisha Stein."

"Aww," Lish beamed. "I can throw my leg back pretty far, huh?"

"Like you could reach out and touch yesterday."

The girls shared a laugh and finished their food. It was truly a great day, and Piper was sure there was no problem a little girl time with your best friend couldn't solve.

CHAPTER 2

He was chasing her, and he was going to catch up. Confronting him was risky; doing it at his house was utterly foolish. Nonetheless, feeling bold, irate, and holding a weapon gave Piper the gusto she needed at the time. The gusto was gone now, replaced with the reality of the pile of shit she was in.

Scott had just exited his car when she ran up to him, pissed and waving the gun. Julia and Ryan were inside, which was good. They didn't need to see this. The husband and father they loved beg for his life.

However, Piper should have known someone was bound to get hurt, and it looked like it would be her. She should have left well enough alone, but revenge called to her.

It all happened so quickly.

"Hi, you piece of shit," Piper said, stepping from the side of the house after Scott had shut and locked his car door.

Momentarily stunned, he took a step back. Slowly his shock turned to anger.

"And just what the fuck are you going to do with that?" he'd asked.

"Retaliation," she said, lifting the gun higher to aim at his head.

Truthfully, she had no idea. She was not a murderer. The point was to make herself feel a little better. However, it was his next words that sent her hands into autopilot.

"You're too stupid to get revenge," then with a wave of his hand, he added. "Get out of here, Piper. I never loved you in the first place."

She moved the gun slightly to the right and fired, aiming to shoot past him and place some fear into him. But instead, it grazed his shoulder. Piper covered her mouth, terrified, and Scott used the delay to dive at her. He was angrier than Piper had ever seen. The predatory look in his eyes assured her he intended to kill her.

He wrestled the gun out of her hands, and in fear for her life, she kneed him as hard as she could between the legs and ran. Piper took off into the trees behind his home. His backyard wasn't fenced in, and it connected to a park with a walking trail.

Behind her, Scott collapsed to the ground, cursing in pain but still holding the gun.

Now, running through the woods, with no weapon and at the mercy of the man she'd shot only a few minutes ago, Piper located a thick tall tree and ducked low behind it, trying to catch her breath.

"Where are you, Piper!" Scott yelled. "We can do this the hard way or the easy way, but regardless you're as good as dead."

With her back as flat as possible against the tree, she took a deep breath and slowly turned to peek around for Scott's location. Leaves crumbled under her hands, and Piper panicked, straightening again so that the tree concealed her body.

What if he heard me? She thought.

It didn't matter. She had to try again to get out of here. Without placing her hands on the ground this time, Piper once again peered around the tree. Scott was straight ahead, looking to the left. He must have heard a sound that he thought came from her because he began to creep in that direction with the gun up.

Piper wasted no time getting out of there. Running forward, her feet heating the dirt and rocks, she unconsciously braced herself for the sudden impact of a gunshot to the back.

When her feet hit the pavement of the walking trail, she ran faster. The loud sound of her shoes created a thumping noise that drowned out everything else around her.

Thump, Thump, Thump.

It is so loud. Why is it so loud?

Thump. Thump. Thump.

"Piper!"

It was Scott, he was gaining on her, and he was going to kill her. Risking a glance over her shoulder, she spun around to see how close he was and fell to the floor.

Her eyes popped open, and her living room ceiling came into view.

Dammit. It was a dream.

She'd fallen asleep on the couch, only a short while ago, while reading over some paperwork for her job.

Knock. Knock

That explained the loud thumping in the dream. Someone was at her door.

"Coming."

A quick glance through the peephole revealed the man she was equal parts excited and nervous to see. Piper licked her lips and swallowed, reflexively tidying her hair and ensuring her comfy shorts and t-shirt were presentable before opening the door.

"Des. Hi."

He smiled at her.

Fuck me now, she thought.

"Hey Piper. Please tell me you finally have some time to talk?"

"I do, come in."

Piper stepped out of the way, and Desmond entered the apartment. He was wearing blue jeans and a dark blue sweater. When he stepped past her, Piper could smell the faint scent of his cologne, and it took her back to the night he'd made love to her. Halting the play by play her mind was setting up, Piper closed the door and turned to face him.

"So, what's up?"

She knew what was up. It was the moment of confession. Now that the time had come, she suddenly realized that she didn't know how to handle this information.

Desmond was a cheater, much like Scott. Did she still want to be with him? Or would this be the end of their friendship? That last question sent an unexpected blow to her heart. She covered her racing thoughts by offering him something to drink.

"No, I'm fine. I've just needed to talk to you ever since that night and haven't been able to."

A faint throbbing between her legs started, simply hearing him mention their time together.

"I know. I came by your place a couple of times, but I got no answer."

"I had to go out of town for work. A major client had important business but desperately needed to continue his therapy. I'm surprised you didn't call," he said, sounding a little hurt.

"I uh, didn't want to bother you."

"Right," he replied, clearly not fooled.

"Well, you could have called me," she said, jumping to defense.

"I could have, but I know you were dodging me, and I wanted to have this conversation in person."

"Oh."

He exhaled and leaned against the kitchen island.

"Piper, I want to apologize. I put you in a bad situation by coming on to you when I know that you have a boyfriend. I just wanted you so fucking bad at the time, I didn't care, but afterward, I realized I might have caused more trouble in your life, and that is the last thing I ever want to do."

Piper frowned. It wasn't what she expected him to say, but it was factual. Or, at the time it was true because, as of now, there was no boyfriend.

"It takes two to tango, Des. I'm a big girl. I knew what I was doing, but I agree with you it was a mistake. You have a girlfriend, and I should have never let things—"

"Wait," he said. "I have a what?"

"A girlfriend."

His brows shot up.

"That's news to me."

"Des, I know Legs is your girlfriend. You don't have to pretend."

"Legs?"

Piper grinned a little.

"Sorry, I mean the girl with the long legs I've seen you with a few times. She comes to your house with food, and you walk her to her car."

Shut up, Piper! Now, who sounds like a stalker crazy chick.

"That's fucking disgusting. Legs, as you call her, is not my girlfriend; she's my sister."

"But I saw you hugging her and . . ."

Now that she thought about it, that hug was innocent. It was her mind that had romanticized it.

"You don't hug your family?" he asked.

"I do," she said, overcome with embarrassment.

"You could have just asked."

"Yeah, but assuming was less complicated."

Desmond didn't say anything as his eyes traveled over her body. At this rate, touching her wasn't necessary. His hungry gaze was awakening all the right places just fine.

When his eyes landed back on hers again, he said, "I'm going to go. I hope we can still be friends."

"You don't have to," she said playfully.

"I think I do. My thoughts aren't very friendly right now." He cleared his throat. "I'll see you later, Piper."

Desmond took a step towards the door, and Piper stepped into his path.

"Tell me what you were thinking," she probed.

Deja Vu hit her. A similar conversation is how things unfolded the first time. Desmond chuckled and looked down at her.

"Piper. I really think it's best if I go."

In response, she pulled her shirt off and dropped it to the floor.

"Do you think it's best now?"

She could see the internal struggle in his eyes.

"I think that we aren't doing this. As bad as I want you, and trust me, it's bad, I'm not sharing you with your boyfriend. I'm too greedy for that."

"Lucky me," she said. Good thing I no longer have a boyfriend."

His response was instantaneous.

"Then why aren't you naked?"

Before she could respond, before she could move, hell before she could even blink, he had her in his arms and on the kitchen island. Clothes got tossed everywhere as they both undressed, in between, fervent kisses.

"I missed you," she said.

It wasn't her intention to be so naked with her emotions, but moments of true passion and vulnerability were a funny thing.

"You never have to again," he assured her.

Gliding his fingers over her pussy, he spread her open and put only the tip of his dick inside.

She locked eyes with him.

"I want more."

"Like this," he teased, sliding in further.

The anticipation of feeling him fully inside caused her pussy to throb against him.

"Des, stop it."

He ignored her frustrated plea.

"Do you know what I want, Piper?"

"For me to kill you for testing me? "

He brushed a long, soft curl from her face.

"I want to see how long you can hold out from cuming."

She laughed, her breathing increasing and the wetness from her pussy already coating his dick.

"I can hold out. I've done it before," she said, leaving out the small detail that that attempt was a miserable fail.

"You tried."

"And I'll try again."

"Good," he replied and pushed deep inside.

Immediately Piper clung to him. She would lose this challenge that was no secret, but trying not to would still be fun. Desmond's thrusts shifted effortlessly between slow and fast, dismantling all her willpower. The sensual touch of his hands and lips, setting a trail of fire all over, sent her mind reeling.

How was this man able to penetrate not only her body but her mind? Piper was coming apart at the seams, having him but still needing more. Wrapping her legs around his back, Piper drew closer, bracing herself on her hands to rock back and forward and match his rhythm.

He grabbed her chin and held it in place, licking and lightly biting her lower lip. Piper moaned into his mouth, blissfully taken by his demanding movements. Grabbing hold of the back of his neck, she kissed him wherever she could reach. Her sensitive nipples brushed up against his chest, coaxing endless shivers and screams from her.

Damn, she was going to cum, but she wasn't ready. It would be over, and she never wanted this to end.

"Fine, Piper thought. *"Two can play at this game."*

Adding her flexibility skills to the mix, Piper leaned back and lifted her legs into a V position.

"Shit!" Desmond grunted, clearly feeling the effects of her repositioning trick. "I see you're trying to hang in there, but it won't work."

He slid his thumb over her clitoris and began to massage it. Piper gasped and gripped the sides of the island. This was intense, and trying to pull back was pointless. Desmond only tightened his hold and moved faster.

"Damn you," she panted.

"Don't fuck with me," he growled. "I'm a master at this."

And then it happened. The damn broke, the shivers came, the screaming, begging, and weakness overtook her body.

"There it is," he whispered into her ear, "I love that sound."

CHAPTER 3

Piper had to summon the courage to do this. Jake was playing with his toys which would keep him busy for another 15 minutes tops, and speaking with Jasmine was crucial. Her finger hung over the send button.

What if Jasmine wouldn't talk to her? It was apparent Scott was a sore subject with the woman, and now Piper wanted some of her time.

"But you still have to try," she said aloud.

Pushing the button for Lancer Communications, she sat down at her kitchen table and fidgeted with her work folder.

"Lancer Communications, this is Jasmine. How may I help you?"

"Um, hi, this is Piper, the girl that called the other day looking for Scott."

Jasmine's voice adopted a cold, blunt tone when she said, "Why are you calling me again?"

"I really need to talk to you."

"If you can't tell me where he is, I have nothing to say. Don't call me again."

"Wait! Please don't hang up. I need your help. It seems

Scott played me too."

There was silence on the other end. Piper was confident Jasmine was going to hang up, then the woman cautiously whispered, "What are you talking about?"

Piper rushed to say one of the many horrible truths she believed would hold Jasmine on the line.

"I recently ran into his wife."

Jasmine's voice changed entirely, from hushed and irritated to shocked.

"Into his who?"

"His wife, Julia. Let me guess you thought she was deceased."

"Yeah, I did."

"Well, she isn't. I ran into her a few days ago at my new job, no less. I recognized her from the pictures instantly."

"That bastard. I don't even know why I'm surprised. He lied about so much. Why wouldn't he lie about that too? I was so stupid," Jasmine seemed to say more to herself than Piper.

"Join the club. That's why I need to talk to you. Are you free on Friday, say around 8 pm? I'm speaking with Julia at my place. Maybe we can all talk, and you can help us fill in some of the blanks?"

Piper held her breath. This newfound information could push Jasmine further away. Truthfully, Piper wouldn't blame her. Not wanting to have anything to do with Scott was best for everyone's mental health.

"I'm available Friday," she finally said.

Piper felt such relief. They exchanged information, and as soon as they said goodbye, Jake came over, tapping Piper repeatedly to say he was bored and hungry.

"I can play a few games with you. What about the one you like where we match the cards up?"

"I guess," he replied, less than inspired. "When are you

getting the cartoons back?"

"It should be very soon, Jake. I promise."

"Okay. What about food? I'm hungry."

"Good question. I have a treat for dinner that you will enjoy."

His eyes got big, and the volume of his voice increased several notches.

"What surprise?"

"It's—" she was interrupted by a knock on the door.

She gave Jake an enthusiastic smile.

"I think that might be it! Go to the kitchen table. I'll be right back."

Jake ran to the table, tripping on his way there. He jumped up and said, "I'm okay."

Piper laughed and opened the front door. Des stood there holding two bags of food from McDonald's. He immediately leaned down to kiss her.

"You're just in time. Jake was telling me he was hungry."

She took the bags and gave him a grateful smile.

"Glad I could help," he said.

"Yes, especially since you didn't have to."

"Don't start with me, Piper. I know I don't have to. I wanted to. Did you speak with her?"

"Yes, and she agreed to talk to us tomorrow."

"That's good news."

"It is but, now I'm nervous about what all I'm going to find out from her and Julia. Who exactly is Scott?"

"That I can't help you with, but you know if you need me, I'm there."

"Did you want to join Jake and me for dinner? Or do you still have work?"

"Yeah, I have to get to the rehabilitation center for a client, but I expect you to let me take you to dinner on Saturday."

"I'm looking forward to it."

They kissed again, and it was hard to pull away, but reluctantly she did and closed the door.

Jake was thrilled with dinner, and Piper was thrilled with Desmond. She had no expectations of him, but he surprised her at every turn. A few nights ago, after their steamy sex session, Piper relaxed in his arms while they talked.

The conversation started with Desmond asking her what had happened with Scott. She assumed he was only being nice and didn't really want to hear heavy details, so she gave him short responses to every question. However, after he told her all of her quick replies wouldn't suffice, Piper broke down and told him the whole story.

Desmond was upset and protective, which Piper didn't expect. He didn't yell or shout, but his body language and the fact that he kept referring to Scott as "that piece of shit I better not see" clued her in.

After telling him about running into the wife and Jasmine, she admitted her nervousness to contact Jasmine again because the first time didn't go so well.

"When are you contacting her again?" he had asked.

"On Thursday, the day before I meet with Julia. Jake will be here, and I think that will help my nerves. It's hard to stress about future conversations when you have to stay alert for a rambunctious kid."

"You want me to come by? I have assignments for work, but I can at least give you support during the call."

"No. I'll be fine."

"You don't seem like it."

"I can't believe I loved a manipulative liar like that."

He took her hand and kissed it. "It's not your fault."

"But it is. It has to be. He set the trap, and I fell into it so easily. Now I have to reach out again to a woman that I've never met to get answers to questions that I never knew I needed to have."

She exhaled, reminded of just how ridiculous and pathetic this situation was.

"And there is nothing I can do for you?"

Piper shook her head.

"I'll tell you what. You said you're keeping Jake that day. What are you two having for dinner?"

"I don't know. Normally I cook something."

"I'll bring both of you dinner, and that's one less thing you have to worry over. What would you like?"

Piper's knee-jerk reaction was to decline again but, she could see in his eyes he wanted to help in any way he could.

"That would be nice. Jake loves McDonald's."

She smiled at the memory, and now Jake was sitting at the table relishing in his food. He had a chicken nugget in each hand and the biggest grin on his face. Seeing Jake content always made Piper feel better. People deserved to be happy, and Piper wasn't sure of what the future held, but right now, she was happy too.

"Jasmine, are you there?"

"I'm here."

Piper adjusted the phone so that the speaker faced where she and Julia sat. Julia hadn't said much since she arrived, but Piper could tell she was tired. Her eyes looked like she'd spent the time since they met crying nonstop. Piper wanted to ask about Ryan, but it felt inappropriate. Julia didn't know her, and bringing up Ryan, no matter how pure the intent, could make things rocky. So instead, Piper offered the woman something to drink, but Julia declined.

23

"Alright, Jasmine, Julia is also here, and I . . . I don't know how to start all this."

"Learning why my husband is a lying sadistic asshole is where we should start," Julia said.

Piper turned in her direction. She wanted to comfort her, but again it felt strange. This whole situation was eerie. The wife of the man she was in love with, sitting in her living room talking about it.

Maybe Lish was right. A fight would probably break out.

"I can agree with that," Jasmine chimed in.

"I guess we've found common ground," Piper responded. "Julia, do you want to ask us anything? Or start?"

It only seemed fair for Julia to lead. After all, she was legally tied to him, which meant she'd been played the most. In Piper's opinion, not being Scott's wife was a blessing in itself.

Julia adjusted in her seat.

"I have known Scott for six years. I met him at a bar when I was 23, and he was 24. At the time, he was a bartender. We felt an instant connection and got married ten months later. Admittedly it was fast, and my parents begged me to wait, but I was confident he was the guy for me. Anyway, things were okay for a few months until I found texts between him and his ex one night. He swore she was simply having difficulty letting go and that he loved me and only me. I loved him too, so I accepted his answer, and we moved on.

She paused, taking a second to look away from Piper.

"I eventually found out he was lying, and they were still involved. I left him for close to eight months, but after all his begging me to come back and swearing it was over, I returned. I convinced myself that it wouldn't happen again, but I'd be lying if I said it didn't remain in the back of my mind. After that, life took off, my mom got sick, a couple of years later, I got pregnant with Ryan, and I started working longer shifts at the hospital to earn more money. There was no time to worry about gut feelings or marital issues."

"That's why you didn't seem surprised when I confronted you?" Piper asked.

"Basically," Julia said quietly. Then she looked up. "He really told you both I was dead?"

Piper nodded, and Jasmine verbally confirmed. There was another brief silence. Navigating through this uncomfortable situation was not going to be easy at all.

"I'll have that drink now," Julia said to Piper. "Preferably something with alcohol."

"Of course, Piper said, standing. She found the bottle of wine Lish had left a few weeks back and poured Julia a cup and then decided to pour one for herself. Piper gave Julia a glass, then placed her own on the coffee table.

"May I ask you a personal question, Julia?" Jasmine said.

Julia gulped her wine and threw up a hand.

"Why not? You've probably seen my husband's dick more times than I have."

"I'm not trying to point fingers or anything, but wasn't it weird that you hardly ever saw your husband?"

Julia laughed to herself.

"I thought he was working. Taking care of a house, a child and a sick parent was expensive. I was doing my part by picking up more shifts at the hospital. He has a cousin, Jacob, who lives out of town and owns a construction business. He offered Scott an opportunity to help him run it and make some good money. The only catch was he might be gone two or more weeks at a time. I never knew when to expect him, but we spoke almost every night, and he was bringing home money for bills, along with random gifts, and telling me how much he loved me."

"Does Jacob even live in Milwaukee?" Jasmine asked.

"He does. Scott used to go up there a lot to hang out with

him?"

"So, if you would have called his cousin, Scott's entire plan might have fallen apart?"

"No," Julia said. "I hate Jacob. He's a liar and a pig."

She took another sip of wine.

"I guess Scott is too, just more charming about it. Anyway, they likely would have covered for each other."

"Wow," Jasmine said, "he played that situation to his advantage."

Julia nodded and then said, "I'm not ready to hear it, but how did you meet Scott, Jasmine?"

The pain and hesitation were evident in her voice.

"Almost two years ago at a coffee shop."

"What ended things between you two?" Piper asked.

They heard some movement in the background on the phone before Jasmine continued.

"Sorry, I had to grab something to drink as well. It looks like it's going to be a long night."

There was the sound of liquid pouring into a glass, and a few moments later, Jasmine was back and ready.

"Uh, where do I begin? So many things occurred between us that drove us apart, but ironically, the final nail in the coffin with Scott and I happened when I caught him cheating. I came home early, and he was in bed with a psycho bitch I worked with. He'd come to my job a few times, and they seemed a little too friendly, but you know Scott, swearing it's nothing and making you think you're the crazy one."

"That is ironic. Did you suspect anything beforehand? Were there any signs?" Piper said.

I guess there were always signs he was cheating or could be, but I brushed them off."

Jasmine paused before continuing.

"I know this is hard for you, Julia. I want to kill him, and he isn't even my husband."

"Yeah," was the only word Julia said into the wine glass as she took another giant gulp.

"In the beginning, I thought Scott was the perfect guy. Now that I look back, I notice maybe he was a little too perfect. It was as if he learned all the right things from movies or those 'how to make her fall madly in love' magazine articles. He told me that he worked in Atlanta and was only in Milwaukee one week a month but didn't want that inconvenience to stop us from building something. He also shared that he had a son named Ryan who was cared for by his grandparents and a hired nanny when he was working."

Julia jumped to her feet.

"That is a fucking lie! My mom can't even sit up on her own. How could she take care of Ryan?"

Piper stood as well in an attempt to calm Julia.

"We know. Scott lied to us all. We are only here trying to get to the bottom of this."

Julia faced away.

"This was a bad idea. I should go."

Jasmine remained quiet, but Piper wasn't so ready to throw in the towel. She needed answers, and Julia needed to know who she was married to. If not for her own sake, for her son's.

"I understand, Julia, but please don't go. You, more than any of us, need to hear the truth. You *deserve* the truth."

Julia blinked a few times, trying to keep the tears at bay.

"You've already come this far. Let's just put everything on the table, and you never have to see or hear from either of us again."

"I can agree to that," Jasmine said.

Julia slowly sat down and crossed her arms. Sitting through this Scott reveal session took all her strength, but she tried to hold her composure.

"Did you ever visit where he lived in Milwaukee?" Julia asked.

"Only once. It was a small house that he said he shared with another guy. I lived alone, so my place was more private. We usually stayed here."

Julia didn't comment, so Piper stepped in with a question of her own.

"You said that there were always signs he could have been cheating. What did you mean?"

"Only that he had the chance to, you know? Visiting one week out of the month, being secretive with the stuff he kept in that damn bookbag he carried around that I gave him from my job, by the way."

That last part really seemed to piss Jasmine off.

"The whole relationship was stupid. I thought Scott cared about me, so I did whatever I could for him. The first time things got out of line was when he showed up with a broken arm from falling off a ladder at work."

Piper's stomach lurched.

This was all a game to him. A sick, twisted and selfish game.

Jasmine pushed on, her next words identical to what Piper had done.

"I let him stay with me a few days, and that's when he began becoming possessive over what I did. I would come home from work and, he'd be sitting on the couch. The next thing I knew, he was giving me the third degree."

Jasmine deepened her voice to imitate Scotts before moving on.

"You only work 15 minutes away. Why does it take you so long to get home after your shift is over? Or, I think it's best if you tell your friends not to call you after 9 pm."

Julia laughed to herself. It was a bitter laugh that held no real humor.

"Yup, that's Scott."

"Well, that's when all the arguing started. But because I still, um, loved him," Jasmine stated, the words a lot quieter than the rest. "Instead of pulling away, I tried to get closer. I wanted to prove my love and get him to understand that nothing had changed between us."

"I know what you mean," Piper commented. "Arguing but wanting to keep holding on."

"Yeah, well, it only escalated from there. One night we went out to dinner, and when the check came. He said he'd left his wallet, and I ended up paying for it. It was no big deal, but after that, money issues kept occurring, and eventually, I was giving him close to $1,000 a month."

"Shit!" Piper yelled, almost falling off the couch. "He did that exact thing to me!"

"Wait, let me get this straight," Julia finally cut in. "He was getting money from both of you?"

"Looks like it," Jasmine said.

"Not exactly," Piper answered. "I didn't have much money to give because I was going through my own financial drama."

"Unfortunately, I'm a saver, and I did have money to help him, and that's what I did, but it didn't fix anything. He only seemed to get more possessive over what I did or why I did it."

"He's crazy. That has to be it," Piper said.

Julia remained silent. She seemed to be in deep thought.

"I think you're right. I found him talking to himself in the mirror one day, saying he needed more time to set his plans. When I asked, "what plans?" he played it off and accused me of hearing things."

"Scott is bipolar," Julia quietly inserted.

There was silence from Jasmine and Piper.

"I found out after we were married a year. He's on meds for it and sometimes has highs and lows. He does these peep talks to himself. I think it's his way of working through stress."

"Well, does his dick have highs and lows too? Is that why he is running around putting it in everyone? Because it's stressed!" Piper snapped.

"What is that supposed to mean?" Julia asked.

"That piece of shit, aka your husband, is playing on people's emotions, and it sounds like you're defending him."

"I wasn't defending him. You took it that way."

"I only took it that way because you said it that way."

Jasmine was saying something in the background, but neither Julia nor Piper were paying her any attention.

"Don't put words in my mouth."

"Don't say stupid shit," Piper retorted.

'LADIES!" Jasmine shouted. "The enemy here is Scott. You know, the guy who has literally fucked everything. The man who is telling the world you are dead, Julia. He is the problem, not us."

Julia stared at Piper, and Piper closed her eyes. The evening was not supposed to go like this; they were all preyed upon by an unstable predator. Jasmine was right. Directing their anger towards each other would not help matters.

"I need another drink," Piper said. "This is . . . this is a lot, to say the least."

"I need another too. I'm too upset to hear this without alcohol," Julia said.

Piper grabbed the bottle and returned with it. She poured more into her cup and then gave Julia the bottle. The woman filled her glass, took another giant gulp, and sat back.

Jasmine cleared her throat. "Shall I go on now? I'm getting to a part that I think you both will want to hear."

"Yeah," they said in unison.

"Okay, so I started getting suspicious and decided to

search through some of his things. What I found not only pissed me off but confused me more. I planned to dig further, but the cheating incident happened before I got the chance, and I ended up kicking them both out, not too gently, may I add, and I never heard from him again."

Piper and Julia both leaned forward.

"What did you find?" Piper asked.

"I found a folder with bank statements in it. Scott is loaded, or at least he was. The account had over a quarter-million dollars in it, but not too long ago, he must have withdrawn it and placed it somewhere else because the ending balance on one of the statements showed $5."

"Do you remember the bank?"

"Sorry, I don't remember. For one thing, I was rushing because he was in the shower. Also, I was upset by the amount. Here I was helping him, and he had more money than me. The other thing I came across was a second cellphone. I did a quick search and found tons of women's phone numbers in there."

"I'm married to a monster," Julia said.

She was speaking to herself again, not seeming to care that Piper and Jasmine were listening.

"How did this happen? For years we've struggled financially. I've worked non-stop to do my part in keeping us afloat, and he's had the money. Daycare, medical bills, past-due mortgage payments, endless car repairs, student loans, he could have fixed it all."

A tear rolled down her cheek.

"Umm, maybe we should pick another night to talk more," Piper gently said.

"NO! I want to hear what else this bastard has done. Jasmine, go on."

Her sudden outburst impressed Piper. Julia had finally found her fury.

"There isn't much to add because, as I said, shortly after, I caught him cheating with a girl from my job. I never heard from him again, but I sure did hear from her."

The hairs on the back of Piper's neck stood.

"What do you mean?"

"She called, saying I better stay away from Scott or else. I told her if she ever called my phone again, the next time she would see Scott is when he joined her in hell because I would end her. She never called again."

"And that worked?" Piper asked.

"It had no choice but to work. I knew where she lived, and I am good friends with the manager. I could have gotten her fired."

"I think that is the same girl that has been harassing me. She called me saying the same thing. What's her name?"

"Vanessa, and I'm almost positive it's her. She's 22, completely off her rocker, and head over heels in love with Scott. The only reason I know this is because another woman Vanessa used to share all her business with still works there. She would tell me all the crap Vanessa called and told her. But as long as she didn't bother me again, I couldn't care less. Scott is a disease I want no parts of."

"You may no longer need to kill her, but I do. That bitch sliced my tires, posted my phone number as a sex line, and left a packaged bloody pad on my doorstep. I want to murder her. Where does she live? I can catch the next flight to Milwaukee."

"That's horrible," Julia and Jasmine said.

"I'd want to kill her too, Piper, but I'm sorry. Last I heard from the lady at work, Vanessa moved to Atlanta to be closer to Scott. I told you, she's stupid over him."

Piper pondered Jasmine's response. That meant Vanessa was possibly nearby, and that little fact made Piper smile. She now had the name of the girl that she was going to strangle.

"I wonder why she never called me?" Julia said, perplexed.

"I'm guessing she only got her hands on one of his phones, and more than likely, it was the main one. I did a quick scroll through the second phone I found in his bag, and the last few calls came from Simone. When we first started dating, he told me that Simone was Ryan's nanny, but who knows, Scott lies so much."

"Simone? That's my middle name!" Julia exclaimed. "Wait, so either he tells women I'm dead or in passing that I exist, but as the nanny?!!"

Julia was evidently pissed. Her jaw was clenched, and her fist tightened on the arm of the couch.

"I'm taking that fucker for everything. He will not get away with this."

Julia was shaking her head nonstop ever since she arrived. Up until now, she was handling all of this pretty well. The goal was to hear the truth and details of what her husband was up to in her absence. Cheating was expected, but Piper guessed that never in Julia's wildest dreams did she think Scott could go this far.

Piper and Jasmine were quiet for several minutes; they didn't know what to say. Watching and listening to a stranger practically fall apart in front of you was disheartening, as well as awkward.

"How do you want to proceed, Julia?" Piper finally asked. "Do you not want to hear any more? Or do you need a few minutes?"

"I have no idea. I want to be strong and hear everything you both have to say. But also want to call Scott, lure him home and beat the shit out of him."

Those were Piper's, and likely Jasmine's, sentiments exactly. However, they were done with Scott. Julia still had to face him. They had a child together. Which meant her exit with this deranged man wouldn't be so cut and dry. Piper may have been angry for being played, but at the very least, she was grateful to not be in Julia's shoes.

"When was the last time you spoke to him?" Piper asked Julia.

"Earlier today. I haven't seen him in a couple of weeks, though. I've been trying to be as normal as possible when talking to him since we talked in your office that day. I didn't want to raise his suspicions, I like all the information before I react."

She did that pitiful laugh again, then added, "Where was that logic before I married him?"

"We all were naive when it came to Scott," Jasmine said.

"Yeah, but I was the only one simple-minded enough to marry him. When is the last time either of you heard from him?"

Piper answered first.

"A week or two. We argued the last time, and I told him it was over."

"Months for me. Scott knows not to call me. He has stolen too much money."

Julia held up her third glass of wine for the evening and looked at it.

"I'm going to finish this drink, and then Piper," Julia said on a giant exhale. "I want you to tell me your story with Scott."

The girls sat in silence while Julia drank the remaining wine in her glass. Piper was about to start speaking when Julia held up a finger, poured a little more wine, quickly tossed it back, and then said, "Go ahead."

"Well," Piper began. My story isn't that long. It mirrors what you and Jasmine had to say. I met Scott at the airport, and I thought something magical was beginning. He spent months laying the foundation to prove he was a good man with my best interest in mind. Only to start gradually showing me a different side and making me feel like every-thing was my fault. We had rifts through the relationships here and there, but I truly realized that I didn't know Scott when I called Lancer Communications looking for him. "

"I'll bet his lying ass doesn't work anywhere," Jasmine interjected. "With all the stealing and elaborate schemes he comes up with, he's just living off unsuspecting women. I'm glad I didn't sign my name to anything for him. A few months before I caught him with Vanessa, he asked me about cosigning on a new car."

"I don't know why he needs a new car. I cosigned for his current vehicle last year," Julia said.

At this point, her voice sounded flat and unaffected. Maybe the wine was finally numbing her emotions.

Suddenly Piper thought of something. She went to her bedroom and grabbed an envelope that had come for Scott. Up until this very moment, she had completely forgotten about it. Piper studied it for a few seconds before ripping it open, not giving a shit that it was a federal offense. Who was going to report her, Scott?

She pulled out a folded piece of paper and opened it, then began laughing, really laughing. This man, this liar, this bastard had balls bigger than the ones she remembered seeing.

"What's funny?" Julia asked, turning around.

Piper walked over and passed one of the small square sheets of paper to her. It took Julia a second to understand what she was looking at, but then she got it. Her eyes widened, and her response was to grab her wine glass and drink some more; obviously, she needed more numbing.

"Hey, Jasmine. Missing any checks?" Piper asked.

"Huh?"

"Scott had something mailed to my place a few weeks back. He never picked it up since we were in a fight, and I'm guessing he forgot about it. Its blank checks that belong to you."

"What the hell?! What's the bank name on them?"

There was movement in the background that sounded like Jasmine was walking quickly through her house.

"Boulder Point Credit Union."

"He stole my checks! I'm looking in my drawer now, and some of the checks for my savings account are missing. I guess he was going to forge my signature and hope I wouldn't notice.

"Yeah, but how would that work? Eventually, you'd find out, especially if he was depositing it into his own account."

"Maybe it would be my word against his, or he planned to have psycho Vanessa deposit them and then leave her high and dry after he got the money. Julia, your husband, is the devil's spawn."

"I'm finding that out."

"What are you going to do?" Piper asked Julia.

"Besides divorcing him and taking him for all he has, I'm not sure. I want to confront him, but first, I'm going to consult with a lawyer and gather all the necessary evidence I need. If I spook him, he might disappear."

"That's a good plan," Piper said.

She was glad that Julia was going to stand up for herself. The woman deserved better, and so did Ryan. But there was more that needed to be said, and with all the dirty laundry and confessions being aired, there was one last thing Piper needed to do. Getting involved with a married man wasn't her intent, but nonetheless, it happened.

"Julia. For what it's worth, I'm sorry for sleeping with your husband. If I had any idea he was married, I would have stayed far, far away. No one should ever experience what you have."

"I agree," Jasmine added. "I wanted to say something

earlier, but it sounded dumb. I assumed you'd know I wanted no parts of this. However, I'm sure hearing it still matters on some level."

"It does, and I appreciate it. But I think the only thing that will really make me feel better is seeing this whole world of lies he created collapse around him."

"Yes, Scott deserves to suffer for what he's done," Piper said. "I won't lie, luring him into a trap and getting some revenge has crossed my mind quite a few times tonight. I don't like people to get away with trying me. But this time, I'm going to be the bigger person and walk away. He's not worth it, and I have so much else to be thankful for."

Piper's mind traveled from her amazing best friend to her fun-loving and supportive cousins Chloe, Talia, and Russell, to her new job and ultimately landed on Desmond. They had dinner plans tomorrow night, and she could not wait.

"Dammit! I'm way up here and have to listen from the sidelines. Just do me a favor, when Scott does get the rug pulled from under him, please, kick him one hard time in the dick for me," Jasmine said.

Piper laughed, and then another thought came to mind, a creepy one.

"Um, Julia, do you have a life insurance policy?"

"No. I've been meaning to get one forever but haven't gotten around to it. Why?"

"I saw a life insurance policy with your name on it inside a folder Scott had. Do you know anything about that?"

Julia slowly shook her head. Her wine-induced chill was unable to cover the fear that was forming over her face.

"I think Scott has gotten one started for you without your knowledge."

"But why would he do that, unless he . . . He wouldn't try to kill me, would he?"

CHAPTER 4

Now this is what a check should look like, Piper thought.

She had just finished checking her account balance for her direct deposit and had the biggest smile on her face. If someone walked into her office at that moment, they would think she was a crazy woman, sitting there, grinning like a lunatic. However, Piper did not care; extreme happiness was her entire mood.

Not only was there enough money to pay all her bills, but she could also get a head start on paying Lish and get the Wi-Fi and cable turned back on.

Life was good.

Her cell vibrated on her desk with an incoming call from Lish.

"Why are you up so early?" Piper answered the phone.

"I had to take my sister to a doctor's appointment. I'm currently sitting in the car, bored out of my mind. Then it hit me. Piper is up being all responsible and whatnot. Why not call her?"

"My responsibility has paid off. My check looks fabulous!"

"Yay! What will we be doing?"

"Hold your horses. I'm not going on any shopping sprees yet, but you have some money coming your way."

"I better not. I told you don't worry about it. Besides, I'm just going to spend it on something pointless, like more clothes, jewelry or colorful wigs for my performances."

"Who cares? It's your money to do as you please."

"How about you hold on to it and do me a favor instead?"

Piper sat back in her chair and lowered her voice.

"What have you done that I need to bail you out of?"

Lish laughed.

"Nothing. I ordered more clothes from your cousins over a month ago and haven't gotten it yet."

"Oh, okay. All you have to do is email or call the number on their website. I'm sure they will take care of it."

"Yeah, but I was hoping you could call them. Maybe they will feel bad and throw in a free piece or an additional coupon if you call on my behalf," Lish said.

"I'm sure you don't need me for that."

"Please."

Lish was using her pitiful voice, and Piper had no idea why she didn't want to do it herself.

"Fine, I'll call later today."

"Sweet!"

"You're sad."

"But you still love me," Lish singsonged. "Now tell me, how did the meeting of Scott's women go?"

"Haha, you think you're so funny."

"I am funny. Did anyone get punched?"

"No one got punched. We did learn a lot, though."

"Such as?"

Piper took 10 minutes to give Lish a quick run-through of the events of Friday night. It probably would have proceeded a lot faster if Lish didn't stop her every 30 seconds to yell curse words or ask Piper to repeat things that she deemed shock worthy.

When Piper finished, Lish had to summarize.

"Let me get this straight. Scott is likely a sociopath who has been scamming for years and has probably never been faithful to Julia since she's known him because he's been lying to countless women and stacking money in the process?"

"You got it."

"Damn, if I weren't so upset that he played you, I'd be impressed. It takes commitment and skill to keep up with that level of lying."

"True, but now he has to pay for all of it. I assume Julia is serious about leaving him. She was probably on the verge of doing so for years before they had Ryan, and I think our conversation was the push she needed."

"Good for her. A lot of women never leave their trashy husbands."

"But the one part we can't figure out is why he took out insurance on her. It seems kind of far-fetched that he would kill her."

"Yeah, I mean, wouldn't he have done it already?"

"That's what we were thinking. Knowing Scott, it's probably some scam. I'll bet he is fucking some girl that works for an insurance company and has something up his sleeve."

"No shit, that would be insane. People do commit insurance fraud every day. That sounds right up his alley."

"In the meantime, Julia plans on staying with her best friend. She's still going to go to work, take care of her parents, Ryan and take legal action; she'd just rather not do it at a home she shares with Scott. To cover her tracks, she's going to tell him some lie about not feeling safe in the house alone on the days she comes home since he's gone for such long periods of time."

"On the days she comes home?"

"Yeah, remember, she works extra shifts and stays overnight at the hospital two nights a week? The days are random, but that's how Scott was able to bring Ryan to my house overnight, and poor Julia never knew a thing."

"I forgot about that part. Damn. I'm speechless, and that's a rarity."

"Oh wait, I forgot to tell you the best news. I found out who the stalker bitch is. Her name is Vanessa, and she used to work with Jasmine."

"Just tell me when and where, and we can go visit her."

Piper laughed a little too loud and had to cover her mouth. A few people passing by her office gave her a look as they walked by the open door."

"You are insane. I don't have all that information yet, but I'll let you know when I do."

"You better."

"I will, but I need to get back to work. I'm already ahead in my tasks for the day, and I want it to stay that way."

"Have I told you I don't like this new corporate version of you?"

Piper laughed and ended the call.

There weren't many patient packets to prepare for today since she completed most of them before she left Friday. Therefore, moving on to reviewing files for all the patients with insurance issues was next on her list. Later today, she would need to call the cable company to get her services re-connect and her cousin to ask about Lish's order.

Piper resorted back to her nonstop smiling from earlier as she thought about being able to watch her favorite shows again. Like shopping and nights hanging out in the city, they were outlets for stress that were deeply missed.

The last couple of months before Piper landed the job at Juniper had been all work and hardly any play. It was the roughest patch she'd ever experienced in life as an adult. Thankfully, that season was now ending, and it felt so good to be able to dance through life again, especially since this time, it would be with her clothes on.

Dagger was running in circles at the park, trying to catch a bird. He would get within mere inches before the bird flew away again. This game of chase had been going on for a few minutes, and Dagger seemed oblivious to the fact that he was being toyed with and repeatedly outsmarted by the chirping flyer.

"He's going to get dizzy. Then you'll have to carry him home."

"I will not. I'm going to tell him to walk it off like my coach used to tell me."

"And if that doesn't work?" Piper said, lifting her brows.

"An overnight stay in the park would do him some good."

Piper shook her head and smiled at Des.

"I enjoy talking to you."

"Why is that?"

"You're easy to talk to, and you make me laugh. It's hard not to smile around you."

"I like seeing you smile."

Piper had to look away. Those dark brown, enticing eyes of his, paired with sweet words, would have them doing some inappropriate things in this park. Piper wasn't opposed to the idea of public nudity, but it was daytime, and kids were around. Therefore, she would remain on her best behavior.

"You were telling me about your childhood before Dagger took our attention. You have eight siblings, huh?"

43

"Yup. My parents always wanted a big family, and they got their wish."

"Do you want a big family, too?" she asked.

"I want kids. How many isn't important to me. What about you?"

"I'm with your parents. I'd love lots of kids."

"Does that have anything to do with you being an only child?"

"It does. I never want a child to feel like me. What was it like growing up with so many sisters and brothers? I always assumed that would be fun."

"Challenging. One minute it's great because you've always got someone to talk to or play games with when you're bored. The next, it's annoying as hell because everyone has to take a shower, and you're always the one left with no hot water."

"That's not horrible."

"Have you ever taken a cold shower?"

"I can't say that I have. But if that's your only complaint, then it wasn't so bad."

"I was the seventh of nine kids, so that put me pretty far from being the oldest. I had to endure constant fighting to be heard, lack of privacy, never having a say in the games we played or shows we watched, having to sleep with someone's elbow and foot in my back or face, and so on and so on."

"Okay, maybe that isn't always so wonderful. It sounds like you hated it."

"Actually, it was fun. When I was a kid, it was torture sometimes, but I appreciated them more as I got older, and the time we spent at my grandparents' 25-acre farm gave us time to spread out. We are all pretty close now. My sister Raquel, the one you refer to as "Legs" is two years older and has always tried to take care of me. If I ever did get TV time, it was because of her."

Piper leaned back to examine Desmond's physique and then shook her head. The guy was built like a Mack truck.

"No offense but, I can't imagine someone needing to take care of you."

Desmond laughed.

"Well, Raquel's issues are deeply rooted. I was a scrawny, quiet kid and got picked on a lot because of it. Raquel was always ready to step in and fight anyone that tried to mess with me. Then when I was seven, I had to get my tonsils removed, and she barely wanted to leave my side."

"Aww, that is sad but extremely adorable that she loved you so much."

"It was. Since we are close in age, we did a lot of things together, and I guess no matter how old I get or how many pounds I can bench press, she will only see me as the baby brother she walked to school."

"You're going to make me ruin my mascara."

"You'll still be beautiful to me."

She nudged him.

"Stop trying to get lucky, Mr. Ash."

"I only speak the truth, but if it gets me another taste of you, I'm all for it."

She touched his face and gently ran her fingers over the light stubble beard. Next, she placed her lips on his and kissed him tenderly.

Dagger ran over and barked at them. The bird was gone, which meant no more interest in outdoor time.

"I guess we'd better get going," Piper said.

"Before we do, I need to ask you something."

"Sure."

"You remember my friend, William, the chef?"

"Yes, of course."

"He's having another cooking class, but this time it will be a contest. The best team wins a $200 gift card to the restaurant of their choice. Would you be interested in entering with me?"

"Just tell me where and when, and I'm there."

Desmond stood and extended his hand. Piper placed hers in his, and Desmond pulled her to her feet. They kissed again briefly before he slid his arm around her, and they took the short walk back to their apartment building.

Once home, Piper stripped off her clothes and jumped in the shower. She would have invited Desmond to join her, but he had an early morning the next day, and she didn't want to interfere. Besides, it's not like she didn't have work as well.

It wasn't clear what she and Desmond were or if they would ever be anything. At present, all Piper wanted was the calming escape his presence offered.

Much too often, the thought of Scott still flooded her mind, and the affliction brought on by his actions left her holding a bag of negative emotions too heavy to carry. His cunning and cruel ways made her feel inept at choosing a good man.

Is Desmond a good man? Or do I just want him to be?

She had given Scott almost a year of her life and was left with nothing good to show for it. It still baffled her how someone could look into your eyes day after day and deceive you. Knowing that she meant nothing to him all this time pissed her off all over again.

Making him pay for what he'd done would be so easy. She could lure him into a trap and then whack him upside the head. When he was unconscious, she could hang him by his balls. The thought was comical and revealed that maybe she hadn't outgrown her desire for petty revenge after all.

At least she hadn't heard from psycho girl. Then again, Scott also hadn't reached out, which was likely why Vanessa kept her distance.

Just as Piper exited the shower, she heard her phone vibrate on the nightstand.

"Speak of the fucking devil," she said.

It was a message from Scott stating that he was sorry for being an asshole and wanted her back. Automatically Piper began to type out a reply.

You worthless piece of . . .

She erased the message. Responding was pointless and unnecessary. It would only provide Scott with more reasons to lie and Piper with no other choice than to retaliate.

"Let it go, Piper," she said to herself after taking a deep breath.

"Do not engage. He is not worth it."

The phone chimed again, and her ability to be the bigger person had faded. He started this game, and she was more than happy to finish it. Piper lifted the phone, preparing to put him in his place, but the text wasn't from Scott. It was from Lish.

Lish: I know you forgot, but this is your friendly reminder to call your cousin about the order.

Oh yeah, the favor to her best friend had completely slipped her mind. Lish's message was right on time and definitely the distraction Piper needed. There was no time to play childish games with Scott. Therefore, she deleted his message, finished getting dressed, and dialed Talia.

"Hello."

"Hi Talia. This is Piper."

"This isn't Talia. It's Tina. I'm handling all calls right now while she takes meetings."

Piper cursed under her breath. She was not in the mood. The goal was to keep her mind off of killing Scott. Closing that wound by opening another was counterproductive.

"Oh," was all Piper could think to say.

"How've you been?" Tina asked.

47

Piper looked at the phone. Had Tina somehow forgotten that they might have been cousins, but they definitely weren't friends?

"I'm fine, Tina. Listen if you could tell Talia—"

"May I ask you something?" Tina said.

Piper almost snapped at the sudden interruption, but Tina's voice held no signs of mischievous intent. She sat down on the bed and switched her phone to the other ear.

"Sure, Tina."

"Why don't you like me?"

Piper laughed.

"Tina, that was a good one, but I am not in the mood for this, okay?"

"No, seriously, why? I know that we have had a rocky past, but I've changed, and after our last encounter, I don't think you believe me."

"You didn't seem like you'd changed at the party."

"You called me fake that was merely a knee-jerk reaction. I truly have changed, and I meant it when I apologized to you a couple of years back."

"And I accepted your apology."

"But did you, really?" Tina replied, unconvinced.

"I said I did."

"I guess it doesn't help that both of us have tempers."

"That's true," Piper admitted, "But okay, you've changed. I've accepted your apology, and everything is wonderful. I gotta go."

"I wish we were close again," Tina said quietly.

"Tina, we were never close."

"Yes, we were when we were kids."

"When we were kids, you harassed me."

"Only because I thought you were cool."

"If that's how you show someone you think they are cool. You need to take a few lessons in compliments."

"That's fair."

Piper had braced herself for Tina to get angry at her statement, but the levelheaded response was highly unexpected.

Deciding to bring up another point, Piper said, "Let's fast forward past our childhood. When I became a stripper, you said horrible things and looked down on me. Explain that."

"That was jealousy," Tina responded with simplicity.

Piper almost dropped the phone.

"What?"

Tina exhaled and repeated herself.

"It was jealousy."

"Are you saying you wanted to be a stripper?"

"Hell No!" Tina laughed. "I was jealous because you possessed a level of confidence that I never had."

"How could you not have confidence? You are beautiful, and you get all those guys to buy you things, and you don't even have to sleep with them."

"Piper, seriously? You are just as beautiful, but unlike me, you don't hide behind men. You live your life for yourself. Not for the attention, not for the free vacations, and not because of the world's expectations. And here's a little secret. Sometimes, when people see beauty, they think there isn't anything more to you, so they treat you more like a prize than a person. I was too afraid to push back. If everyone else thought I was a nice face and nothing more, maybe they were right."

Piper couldn't believe Tina's words. Was that really how her cousin had felt about herself all these years?

"But you started a business."

"I did, but that was hard. Everyone thought Talia and I were jokes."

"Well, clearly, they were wrong. You both are super talented."

"Thanks. Piper, I really am sorry."

"So am I. Had I known you felt this way a long time ago, it could have saved us years of fighting."

"But we're so good at it," Tina joked.

"We are," Piper agreed with a smile. "That's wild, though, goes to show you never know what's on someone's mind. You seem to have it all."

"I have a lot to be thankful for, don't get me wrong. But I've never even had a serious relationship. I think Talia and I have played arm candy girls so long to men who care about nothing beyond the surface that the thought of getting close to a guy scares the hell out of us."

Piper scoffed, "Trust me, serious relationships aren't as glamorous as people make them out to be. Doing it your way is probably smarter."

"Why do you say that?"

"No reason, just a little drama in my life."

"Like what?"

Piper was silent. She didn't feel uncomfortable talking to Tina about this, but it was unfamiliar territory. Tonight had been their first real conversation in a long time, and it had been good. Piper found herself not wanting to ruin that.

But then Tina said, "I know maybe it's weird to share with me, but I honestly wouldn't mind being a listening ear. Plus, I'm bored waiting for Talia to come back. Please put me out of my misery."

"Are you sure?"

"I am. I haven't been in a serious relationship, but I know men can be some interesting creatures."

"The only interest the guy I was dating had was lying."

"That one I'm familiar with. A lot of the men I meet are hiding something or someone."

"What do you do when they're hiding both?"

"End him," Tina said casually.

"Yup. We're related."

"What exactly did he do?" Tina said. "If you don't mind me asking, I mean. I'll understand if you don't want to share the details."

"You know what, Tina?" Piper said. "Get ready for your boredom to be cured."

Piper spent the next thirty 30 minutes telling Tina all about Scott's world of lies. When she was done, Tina only had one question.

"Why haven't you tied that man up somewhere and left him in a closet?"

"Ugh, don't tempt me. I'm trying to be the bigger person, and it's hard because he deserves to suffer."

"I get that you're trying to be a bigger person. I had to travel that same road, but some people need their asses handed to them."

Piper fell back onto her bed. Scott was some people. He needed his ass, his dick, and his whole existence handed to him and then flushed down the toilet.

"What would you do if you could get back at him?" Tina asked in a voice that sounded like the kind of trouble Piper loved.

"I hadn't spent much time thinking about it because if I do, I'm likely to give in."

"If you need some ideas, I have a few."

Piper would prefer to think up her own revenge plans but felt intrigued to hear what Tina had to say. They were family; just how deep did the similarities go?

"Alright, Tina, what would you do if you were in my shoes?"

Tina was quiet a second while she thought about it.

"You said he kept a lot of secrets, right?"

"Yes."

"Well, a secret isn't a secret if everyone knows."

CHAPTER 5

"I've missed you, Scott. After our last argument, I was so angry and hurt that I thought I wanted you out of my life for good. But I realize we've been through so much I can't imagine being with anyone else. I love you."

"I love you too, Piper. I'm glad you came to your senses. It took you a while this time. What changed?"

Piper rolled her eyes. Thank God they were on the phone, so he couldn't see how annoyed she was.

"I think I just had a lot going on. My aunt, the things with Simone, being low on cash and having to go back to stripping."

"Aww, Baby, I understand, and hey, stripping is what you do, and it pays the bills. If you have to return to it now and again, that's not so bad. I'll be there to cheer you on all the way."

Piper had to bite her tongue and close her eyes to keep from falling out of character. The goal was to get him to dig himself into a deeper hole. Piper thought about all the money he had stashed away.

"I know you will. I wish you could help me. Things are so rough right now."

"Me too, sweetie. We will get through this. Remember, what I have, you have. Unfortunately, I don't have anything right now."

"I understand. You're such a good guy. How did I get so lucky?"

"I'm the lucky one to have a woman like you."

Bile rose in Piper's throat as Scott poured on the fake sincerity. How had she ever let this man touch her? He was heartless scum and deserved a lot worse than he was going to get.

"I'll be in town in a few days. Can I come by?"

"I would love that. I actually have a surprise planned for you."

"Do you now?"

"Yeah. It's been a while, and I wanted us to do something romantic together."

"Romantic sounds like we might not need clothes at some point," he said in a deep voice.

"For what I've got planned, you won't be needing clothes at all."

"I like the sound of that. Does Friday work?"

"I can't on Friday. I need to work late."

"Cleaning out more dog cages, huh?"

For a second, Piper was confused by his comment, and then she understood. Scott didn't know that Piper had a new job. Between all the arguing they did, she never had the chance to tell him.

At the time, that seemed terrible, but now it was a brilliant twist of fate. If Piper had told Scott she was working for the same hospital as his wife, who knows what he would have done to sabotage things.

"Yeah, you know Mrs. Friedman always needs me to do more than my fair share. What about Saturday?"

"I'll have to move some things around, but for you, it's worth it."

"Great! I'm looking forward to it."

That was probably the first honest emotion she had shown this entire conversation.

"Oh wait, do you mind bringing that mail I never picked up?"

"Piper's lip's tightened.

"Sure thing."

"Thanks. Love you, babe."

"Love you too," she managed to say.

As soon as the call ended, Piper screamed. Once she collected herself, she looked up and said, "Did you get all that?"

Tina hit a few keys on her laptop.

"Every word. It's going to be great for the website."

Julia sat next to Tina, doing exactly what she did the last time she was there, shaking her head.

"I still can't believe it," Julia said. I knew he was cheating. I was certain everything you and Jasmine told me was true but hearing it . . . I still don't think I was prepared."

"No one can prepare for something like that," Piper said.

"I guess not," Julia responded, standing to her feet. "I have to be on my way, doing another shift at work tonight. Got to keep up appearances until Scott is officially served."

"Okay. Are you sure you don't want to know what I planned?"

"It's juicy," Tina added.

"No. If this comes up in court, I want to be able to say with total honesty that I had no idea."

She picked up her purse, told Tina it was nice to meet her, said goodbye to Piper, and then left the apartment.

Piper went to sit beside Tina, who had resumed hitting keys on her computer.

"She seems like a nice lady," Tina commented without looking up. "It's horrible what her husband did to her."

"It is. When I asked her if she wanted to hear this conversation between him and me today, I was slightly surprised when she agreed. Scott's actions have already delivered her a lot of pain. I'm glad she came, though."

"Me too. It's always best to hear from the horse's mouth, and now she has."

Tina hit a few more keys and then closed her laptop. Placing it into a pink and gold computer bag, she zipped it up and stood.

"I need to get going too. I will call you if I need anything."

Piper was quiet for several beats.

"Tina, this is a lot. We have barely spoken in years, and now you're pulling favors to help me with my drama. You didn't have to be there for me like this."

"Girl, Please. You are my cousin, my family. The only person allowed to piss you off is me. Anyone else tries it, and they are going to pay."

Piper gave her a knowing smile.

"Is that the only reason?"

"Fine! It's also because I still have a streak of the mean girl in me, okay?" Tina confessed.

"I thought so. Come on. I'll walk you out. I need to check the mail anyway."

Piper walked Tina downstairs to the front door of the apartment building and hugged her. It was a little strange rebuilding their relationship after such an extended period, but it also felt right. One could never have too many family members in their corner.

The thought sent her mind to her cousin Russell. Reaching out to him later was a must on her to-do list. The last time they spoke, he told Piper he was keeping busy to avoid spending too much time feeling depressed about how much he missed his mom.

Tina opened the door to exit and stopped.

"Oh yeah, don't forget to tell Lish that her package will arrive soon, and it will include a complimentary coupon for one free item as an apology for the delay. Twindle has been insane, in a good way. We sent out emails for items that had to go on backorder. I'm surprised she didn't get it."

"She probably did, but Lish never checks her email."

"Gotcha. Well, either way. We've got her covered."

"I'll let her know."

The girls waved another goodbye, and Piper went over to the mail area and opened her box. Inside were three bills and one package. The bills made sense, but the package did not. She hadn't ordered anything, and Lish didn't mention sending her anything.

For a split second, Piper's alarm bells shot up as she recalled the offensive package sent by Vanessa not long ago. Flipping over the thick padded envelope, she studied the delivery address, and an instant calm suppressed her nerves. The package was intended for Vince and placed in her mailbox by mistake.

Hmm, I wonder what this is? I'll bet it's nasty, she thought.

Piper slammed the mental door on her curiosity. Vince and Lacy's gross 'sexscapades' were their business. Climbing the stairs two at a time, she stopped in front of the quirky couple's door. The last time she stood here, things that could never be unseen had occurred. Piper didn't want an encore.

She knocked a few times, and within seconds Lacy was swinging the door open.

"Hi, Piper. How are you?"

Lacy's smile was its usual friendly display Piper had grown accustomed to. However, after seeing her and Vince fucking on the table and their big golden finish, Lacy's smile was the only area on the woman's face that Piper could look at without laughing.

"I'm good. I got a package meant for Vince."

Lacy took the bulky envelope.

"Oh, my Vince is going to be so excited."

"Vince, your package came!" she called over her shoulder.

Piper heard footsteps, and suddenly Vince was visible in the doorway standing behind Lacy. If Piper thought looking at Lacy was hard, she underestimated the awkwardness of this entire neighborly exchange. She didn't dare lift her eyes to Vince's face. Instead, Piper kept her eyes fixed on Lacy's smile.

"I'm getting locked up tonight," Vince said with excitement.

That made Piper look up. Not only was it an odd thing to say, but the level of excitement in his voice begged for questioning.

"That's great," Piper said, utterly confused. Then wondered if there was ever any other way to respond to Vince.

Vince took the package and rushed out of eyesight.

"Locked up?" Piper said to Lacy.

"It's his penis cage," Lacy said unbothered.

DAMMIT! Piper thought.

She'd been sucked in again.

Lacy continued.

"He's been waiting all week for it. I'm glad it finally arrived so he can stop bugging me about finding objects around the house as substitutes. Either way, thanks for bringing it by hun."

Lacy closed the door, and Piper regretted ever moving into the building. Now not only did she have to avoid imagining pee covering Vince's face, but she also had to work diligently to block visions of Vince's penis trapped in a box.

"Where did Dagger get his name?" Piper asked.

Desmond and Piper were sitting inside the cooking area, waiting for the competition to start. It was a Thursday evening, and they left as soon as Piper got home from work.

"I don't know. My younger brother Dante, who Dagger technically belongs to, named him. You remember I told you he went away to college?"

"I do remember that. What is he in school for?"

"Biomedical Engineering."

"That's a new one on me."

"He studies, designs, and develops biological and medical systems for improvement."

"I'm still lost."

"Say, for example, you were going to get an artificial organ put in. Someone has to create, study and make improvements on it. That's where his job comes in."

"That is super interesting."

" I think so too. He loves it, and we are all so proud of him."

Piper felt a slight pang of jealousy. It must have been nice growing up in a family of people that supported each other. She had her aunt and a few cousins, but that was once she got older; having an unconditional support system from birth would have made a giant difference in her life.

"That's something to be proud of. Alright, so Dante named Dagger because he was biased to the letter D, it sounds like."

"If he is, he gets it from my mom."

"Your mom loves the letter D too?"

"Yup and R. All of the boys have names that start with D, and all the girls have names that start with R."

That's cute."

"If you say so, we all hated it. Everyone wished they could have had names more cool and dignified."

"Like what?"

"Dante wanted to be Sir Hardin, Raquel wanted to be Queen Alana, and another of my brothers wanted to be King Fransico."

Piper laughed.

"What is wrong with your siblings?"

"We were kids. My older brother, who was ten at the time, actually liked that his name started with a D, but instead of it being Dylan like my parents chose, he wanted it to be Dungeon. He thought the name made him sound powerful and mysterious."

"You guys had some unique imaginations. Why haven't you revealed yours?"

"It's silly."

"So. I want to hear it."

He glanced at her and shook his head.

"No way. You are going to laugh."

"I promise I won't laugh."

Desmond exhaled.

"Captain Twig and Berries."

Expectantly, Piper broke her promise.

"What was wrong with you?" she said, laughing harder than she had in a while.

"I didn't know it had other meanings. All I knew was Captain Crunch was my favorite cereal because of the berries, and I loved playing outside in my pretend treehouse that I made out of—"

"Twigs," Piper said, trying to catch her breath from laughing too hard.

"Yes, twigs. It took me forever to understand why my parents covered their mouths every time I demanded they address me as Twig and Berries."

"You poor thing," Piper said, wiping at the tears in her eyes.

"Yeah yeah, whatever, I'm not going to forget you broke your promise."

Piper finally composed herself and bit her lip.

"I'm sorry sexy. Do you want me to make it up to you?"

"What did you have in mind?"

"I'd let you put your—"

"Des! Man, you are early," William said, walking towards the front of the room, putting down his bags and jacket."

"We overestimated how bad traffic would be. You remember Piper, right?"

"I do indeed," William said. "It's nice to see you again."

"Same here," Piper agreed.

"Actually, you both being here works out great. You mind helping me set up the stations?"

"Not at all," they both replied, getting to their feet.

"I guess now you can't tell me how you were going to make it up to me later?" He whispered to her.

"No need. I can tell you now."

Desmond seemed intrigued.

"I was going to say I'd let you put your hands on my shoulder and gave me a nice back rub; it's been a long week, Mr. Twig."

"Oh, you're funny."

Desmond pulled her in for a hug and quick kiss before getting their directions from William. Setting up the stations didn't last long, and they finished all ten a few minutes before the competition officially started.

Piper was feeling pumped and ready. In her mind, that $200 award already belonged to her and Desmond. However, when one of the judges announced the two dishes the contestants would be preparing for the evening, Piper's confidence wavered.

The goal was to assign one complicated dish and an easier one to make things fair and fun. The first dish was seared duck breast in a lemon sauce, and the second was a five-cheese lasagna.

Desmond and Piper figured it best if they worked on the meals independently and then came together towards the end for time management purposes. With Piper being less experienced in cooking, Desmond handled the duck, and Piper was responsible for the lasagna.

"You better cooperate this time!" Piper threatened the sheets.

The last time she attempted to make lasagna, it tasted pretty good, but it didn't look picture perfect. The judging process placed heavy emphasis on three key criteria: Execution, Taste, and Appearance.

"No need to threaten the food. You'll do great. Have fun with it." Desmond said.

"Quiet you. The lasagna and I have a rocky past."

He chuckled and placed a few duck breasts in a cold sauté pan. Piper started prepping ingredients for her sauce and prayed that things would go well. Piper had never won a challenge before, and winning this one seemed within the realm of possibility.

Forty-five minutes later, the judges were sampling dishes, and Piper's fingers and toes were crossed. In her opinion, she and Des did a fantastic job. The lasagna played nice and didn't fall apart each time she placed it in the square glass pan and carefully covered them with sauce and cheese.

However, as Piper watched the judges take a slice onto

their plates, her self-criticism soared once again. Desmond's duck looked like it fit the judge's expectations, but her lasagna didn't resemble impeccable artistic cuisine.

Maybe she didn't use enough sheets or poured too much meaty sauce on one layer and not enough on the other.

Once the scores had been tallied, and the judges announced the winners, Piper was astounded that they came in third place. That's when it dawned on her that so much time was spent worrying about her own inexperience, she hadn't noticed how un-chef-like the other competitors were.

None of them appeared to be professionals. As a matter of fact, one team's lasagna barely had sheets or cheese. It was merely a giant glob of meaty sauce.

Walking upfront to collect their $50 gift card and tiny third-place trophies, Piper beamed. She'd had fun, enjoyed time with Des, and learned some excellent cooking tips. It may not have been the win she wanted it to be, but with all things considered, tonight's third place felt like first.

CHAPTER 6

Meetings, admissions, filing, and studying various protocols filled Piper's day on Friday. Gone were the days of one task given at a time. She was no longer the new girl, and the workload had increased tremendously. Nevertheless, Piper still loved it, and her initial self-doubt had fully subsided.

After tossing the last folder on the rack for pickup, Piper checked the time and saw that her workday had officially ended ten minutes ago. Collecting her purse, she locked her office and headed to the car. Before getting home, she would need to stop by the grocery store to pick up a few small items for her picnic with Scott tomorrow.

Scott was about to get a kiss from Karma delivered by Piper. Pinpointing her emotions on this revenge plot was tricky. At one point, she loved Scott, or the Scott she thought she knew, and now he had made it to her enemies list.

It saddened her that this is what that fantastic day in the airport almost a year ago had amounted to—a wife, numerous girlfriends (one of them that belonged in a psych ward), and a bag of lies.

Poor Julia. Poor all of them, actually. But poor Julia the most. Her entire life with Scott was a lie, and worst of all, they had a son together. At least, Julia was ready to face the music. She may not have wanted to hear the details of what Piper had planned, but any future plans she had with Scott were over.

However, Lish and Tina were more than excited to indulge in the details. They even offered extra suggestions to nail Scott to the wall. Piper resisted most of them. Her plan was simple. Get in and get out.

Well, she would. Scott would stay, and if her plan worked out, he would be found later by the police. Envisioning that little detail made her chuckle.

Piper entered the store and located the bread and sliced turkey for sandwiches. Even though she and Scott were not about to have the laid-back romantic picnic he expected, keeping up appearances was important. He couldn't carry an empty basket after all.

After paying for her items, Piper called Des on her way home. He had no idea what she was up to tomorrow with Scott, and it would stay that way.

"Hi, Des. How was your day?"

"It was good. I'm currently grabbing a bite to eat with my sister."

"Is that her?" Piper heard a female voice ask in the background.

"Yeah," Desmond responded.

"Give me, give me."

Piper heard what sounded like Desmond's sister yanking the phone from his hand and catching him off guard.

"Hi Piper, I love my new nickname."

"What new . . . Oh," Piper said with a giggle, "Hi Legs."

"Hi! I'm sure you already know my name is Raquel, but

Legs is fine by me. Especially since my brother is quite smitten with you."

Piper found humor in the use of the word "smitten." Raquel said it in a teasing manner, and she heard Des release an annoyed breath.

"So when are we going to meet?" Raquel asked.

Now Piper was caught off guard and almost missed her turn. Flipping on the turn signal, she slowed to an appropriate speed and made a right.

"I'm not sure," she replied.

"Are you free tomorrow?"

"Raquel!" Desmond said. "Your insanity is showing."

"I'm only trying to get to know her."

"Give me the phone," Desmond responded.

"Fine! Here you, Mr., no fun," Raquel said. Then with a shout, she added, "Bye Piper, it was nice meeting you!"

Piper listened to their sibling bickering with curious interest. You could tell that they were more than siblings; they were also friends. Listening to them was sweet and heartwarming.

"Please ignore her," Desmond said, having reclaimed the phone. "I told you Raquel thinks she's the boss."

"You're smitten with me, huh?"

"You're okay," Desmond answered.

Piper laughed.

"I think you and Raquel's relationship is cute. I'd love to meet her."

"Piper. Don't feel pressured to do that."

"No pressure at all. She sounds fun, and I love fun people."

"I guess that part is true. I'll set something up, but first, I'd like to see you again alone. When are you free?"

Piper caught herself just in time. A chance to see Desmond was preferable to most things, and the word "tomorrow" almost slipped out of her mouth.

However, tomorrow Piper will be busy dealing with Scott.

"Sunday. Does that work for you?" she asked.

"I won't be free until after three."

"Perfect."

"Alright. I'll see you then," Desmond said.

"I can't wait. Tell Raquel bye for me."

"Will do," Desmond said.

Piper swooned at how sexy his voice was. Tiny bolts of erotic electricity sprang to life between her thighs.

"Bye, Piper!" She heard Raquel yell before Desmond hung up.

Piper noticed Scott approaching. He waved as he crossed the walking trail and drew closer to her. The time had come, and Piper tensed. She didn't want him touching her. Anger was attempting to poke a hole in her pretend calm demeanor. It was time to play lovey-dovey when all she really wanted to do was bash him upside the head with a skillet.

Scott looked the same as always. Attractive, charming, and friendly, but something had changed. More than likely, it was her perspective about him. Getting a chance to view his true character made his eyes seem too dark and his smile too much like a predator.

Fortunately, they, or rather she, had decided it would be best to meet at the park. Scott wanted to pick her up, but Piper convinced him that meeting there would be easier.

"Baby, how are you?" Scott asked, finally reaching her.

Piper stood.

"I'm great. Better now that I see you."

She tried to make her smile reach her eyes and her voice as flirty as possible. Scott wrapped his arms around her, and Piper relaxed into the embrace. Next, he lifted her chin and kissed her deeply. Piper almost gagged, but mentally replaying the plan kept her on track.

Pull it together, Piper. All of this will be over soon.

"You look good," she said to him.

"You always look good. I missed you, and Ryan does too. If I'm not mistaken, the other day, I think he said your name."

You piece of shit. Using your own child for your evil plans. I can't wait for your balls to meet my shoe, Piper thought.

Aloud she said, "Oh, that's so sweet. Maybe you can bring him next time?"

"Yes, I will."

He slid his hands over her breast and licked his lips.

"I'd love to see what's under this."

Piper took a step back and wagged her finger.

"No. No. You be good now. We will get to that later. At the moment, I have a picnic planned for us."

She placed her hand into his and pulled.

"Come on, let's go find somewhere quiet."

He nodded, and Piper passed him the basket to carry. She adjusted her purse strap on her shoulder, and Scott placed his arm around her. It took close to 10 minutes but eventually, they located a secluded area to set up.

Scott put the basket on the ground and opened it. Reaching inside, he withdrew a folded blanket and looked down at the remaining contents. Piper took the blanket from him and spread it over the grass.

"Only two sandwiches and two bottles of water? What about dessert?" He asked.

Piper straightened the blanket before removing her shoes and purse and walking closer to him.

"I was hoping you would be my dessert," Piper whispered.

She placed a hand on his dick and began massaging it through his jeans. Scott moaned and placed his hands around her waist. He was enjoying this part of the plan way more than Piper wanted. Releasing him, she allowed her fingers to trail up his stomach to his chest.

"You are so fucking hot, Piper. I don't know if I can wait to have you. I've missed you too much."

Step one complete.

Piper looked around nervously. It was a sunny day with only a slight breeze. Birds were chirping, but she couldn't hear any people talking or moving around. They weren't too close to the trail, which meant any unexpected company was unlikely. Scott buried his fingers in her hair and kissed her again. His hands were busy, touching her everywhere; when he pulled at her green and yellow button-down shirt, she halted him.

"I don't see anyone, and having dessert first wouldn't be so bad."

Scott needed no further teasing. He pulled her close, and they fell down onto the blanket. As their lips touched, Piper once again fought the urge to pull away and slap the shit out of him.

Soon, soon, she reminded herself.

Piper helped Scott pull his shirt over his head and then unbuttoned her own. She was wearing a tank top underneath, and before removing her first layer, Piper made sure Scott's shirt was off and his jeans were down to his ankles.

He sat up and quickly removed his shoes and jeans, tossing them to the side while Piper matched his urgency, removing her shirt and undershirt. When Scott reached around to unsnap her bra, she backed up.

"First, I want to take care of you."

He kissed her neck, shoulders and gradually licked his way back up to her mouth. Piper shuttered, and Scott took her reaction as pleasure, not knowing how far off base he was.

Placing his arms behind his head, Scott leaned back and closed his eyes.

"Have your way with me then."

She gave him a wicked grin and proceeded to remove his boxer briefs.

Now he was completely naked, and for the first time that day, joy etched its way into her heart. Straddling him, she slowly started kissing her way down his chest. Placing one hand on his penis, she moved it up and down, trying to keep him locked into the feel-good trance. Scott was rock hard and ready to get the show on the road.

Piper waited until she was further down his stomach before discreetly sliding her purse over and sticking her hand inside. Locking one hand around the small black object, Piper sat up. The time for pleasure was over now; Scott Bolden was about to feel the pain.

With his eyes still closed, he asked, "Why are you stopping, baby? It's just getting good."

"I think our relationship needs more sparks."

"Huh?"

Scott's eyes popped open just in time to see Piper shove a taser between his legs.

She hit the button and quickly moved back before he kicked her in the side. Scott gurgled and shook as his muscles spasmed, causing his body to tighten. Piper tased him again, this time on the side, and Scott jerked and rolled off the blanket and onto the ground.

"You fucking asshole!" she shouted. "I can't believe I ever loved you. Lying about your wife, stringing multiple women along, pretending to love me, all the while only caring about your fucking self."

With her last words, Piper kicked dirt on him and picked

up her clothes. She got dressed and afterward began to gather Scott's clothes as well.

He seemed to be gaining some movement, or possibly her mind was playing tricks on her. Regardless, she rushed over and gave him another jolt in the ass, then resumed collecting his clothes, the blanket, and her purse, shoving everything into the basket.

For a split second, Piper felt remorse at leaving him naked in the woods. However, after recalling all the deception and misery he'd caused, she tased him again. It was a low-voltage taser. Highly unlikely to kill him, and even if it did, Piper felt justified.

Scott grunted and blinked a few times.

She had truly loved this man, was willing to deal with almost anything for him, and this is how he treated her? Hell No. He deserved no fucking sympathy.

Piper scanned the surroundings, ensuring that nothing was forgotten. Unless you counted Scott, who remained on the ground stiff as a statue with his eyes locked straight ahead.

Piper needed to get going. Lish was waiting in the car, not too far from this area. A few days ago, Piper had found this spot. The hunt to locate somewhere private with Scott earlier was all part of the plan.

Although she needed to hurry away, Piper couldn't resist one last comment.

"Say hi to Vanessa for me."

And with that, she ran toward the car. Along the way, she kept stealing glances behind her to ensure Scott wasn't on her trail. Each time she looked back, no one was there but shaking the Deja Vu of the dream she had wasn't easy.

When Piper located Lish's silver sports car, she jumped into the back, and Lish sped off.

"OMG, Piper, I can't believe you did it. You didn't kill him, did you? Knowing me, I would have tased him to death."

"No, but keeping self-control was challenging."

"I'm proud of you. Scott warranted that punishment. You have all his clothes?"

"I got them all right here."

Piper patted the basket and leaned back to catch her breath. The entire plan had gone off without a hitch, and now it was time for the bonus round.

"We should set his clothes on fire."

"No. His clothes are going to the same place I put my feelings for him."

"Where's that?"

"In the trash. Now shhh, I have to do the last part."

Lish pretended to zip her lips and grinned.

Pulling out her cellphone, Piper cleared her throat and pressed three buttons.

"9-1-1, what's your emergency?"

Speaking fast and adding a note of fear to her tone, Piper said, "I was just in Grisham Park, and I would like to report a man for indecent exposure."

CHAPTER 7

"**T**his is insane," Lish said, navigating through the website that Justin, a friend of Tina's, had created about Scott's secrets and lies.

Piper looked over her shoulder.

"Have you read through the entire "Lies he told," page yet?"

"I'm almost done. I can't believe he even lied about the injured arm!"

Piper sighed.

That fact came out as Piper, Jasmine, and Julia continued their discussion the first night they met. Scott had visited Piper and Jasmine around the same time with an arm cast and a sob story about being hurt at work.

However, a week later, when he went home to Julia, he wasn't wearing one. Julia suspected Scott had used a fake cast that was part of some Halloween stuff they had boxed up in the garage.

Lish continued to scan the computer screen. The website was only three pages: a home screen with Scott's slimy face, a second page listing his lies and manipulations, and a third giving other potential victims a chance to come forward.

If anyone submitted anything, Julia was sending it to her lawyer to sift through. If the lawyers found anything of value, it would join the ever-growing pile of evidence they already had against Scott.

Piper really appreciated the added touch of the website and billboard. Her plan was only to abandon him in the park. Exposing him on a grander scale was Tina's idea. Her friend Justin was a computer tech that worked for a digital billboard company and owed her a favor.

Justin created the billboard ad about Scott and used a space off of 285, a major highway in Atlanta, to display it. The giant advertisement loomed above the popular route with a picture of Scott smiling, and next to it were the words, "A Cheater's Confession."

The public notice directed people to a website to read about Scott and how he schemed four (and likely countless other) women. Both the site and billboard would only stay up for 30 days, but the point was to give him the same embarrassment and betrayal he had subjected them to.

"I still can't believe you left him in the park naked. You should have taken a picture of it."

"Damn! That is a good idea. I was so focused on getting out of there I didn't even think about it."

"Are you ready for breakfast? Because I'm starving."

Lish had stayed the night, and now they were up looking at the site and laughing about the details of the day before.

"Yes, let's eat."

The girls made eggs, pancakes, and bacon. At the last second, they had to add biscuits because Lish was craving jelly. Once they sat down to eat, Piper loaded her plate with food, positioned her fork over a fluffy pile of eggs, and stopped.

"I forgot I have something exciting to do."

"What?" Lish asked.

"I'll be right back."

Piper grabbed her cell phone from the kitchen counter and hurried into her bedroom. Fifteen minutes later, she returned with the biggest smile on her face and a small black booklet.

"I'm all set!"

Lish glared at her.

"Are you going to tell me what you're all set for?"

"To get my cable and wifi back! I'm so happy, and Jake is going to be thrilled."

Lish rolled her eyes and pulled her plate closer.

"I thought you had something juicy to tell me. You were acting all secretive. And what's with the black book?"

"Sorry to get your hopes up, friend. I needed my planner to write down the appointment."

"A planner? You're so old."

Lish took a bite of her buttery biscuit that she had loaded with strawberry jelly. The jelly oozed out the sides, and a glob of it fell onto her plate.

"You should have skipped the biscuit and ate a bowl of jelly instead, Lish."

"Mind your business, planner lady."

"Don't get mad because I'm all fancy now with my sched-uled meetings and deadlines. Don't worry, I penciled you in too for your eight-year work anniversary, see."

Piper flipped the book open, pointed at a date and turned it towards Lish.

"What's LPP?"

"Lish's Pussy Performance."

Lish shook with laughter causing more drops of jelly to fall onto the plate.

"You're silly. So, when are they turning your services back on?"

"Next Sunday at 12. Want to celebrate and watch some medical dramas with me?"

"Will there be snacks?"

"Of course!"

"Then I guess I can kill some time before work."

Piper clapped her hands and poured syrup onto her pancake.

"What are you doing today?" Piper asked, cutting a slice of pancake with her fork.

"Let's see," Lish said, looking up. "I'm going to hang with you until noon, and then I'm going to go see this guy I met last weekend at a private party where I performed."

"Details, please."

"I don't know much about him yet. He approached me after the show and asked me out on a date."

"What does he look like?"

"Average looks, average height, average voice. Nothing to brag about."

"Do you even like him?"

"Not really, but he truly likes me. He offered me an additional $500 that night to sit and talk with him."

"Couldn't resist the pussy, huh?"

"Exactly. You know how it is? Guys, see it on stage and fall instantly in love."

"Yeah, I don't miss that part."

"Do you miss any of it?"

Piper thought about it.

"How sexy being on stage made me feel."

"You don't feel sexy now?"

"I do, but it's a different type of sexy when you're on stage entirely free and drawing the audience in."

"I know what you mean, which is why I still love it? But

not the thirsty guys, who like the idea of me, instead of the real me. I know it comes with the territory, but it gets old."

"Yes. I only wanted to do my dance, empty their wallets and credit cards, then go on about my life. Not hear how much they love me when they don't know me."

"It's business, not personal but—"

"They always make it personal," Piper and Lish said at the same time.

The girls laughed and continued eating.

"So, what makes you feel sexy nowadays?"

"Des."

"Now, those are the details I want. What's going on with you two?"

"Nothing much. A bunch of sex but other than that, we're taking it slow."

"Do you love him?"

"No," Piper answered truthfully. "I'm still recovering from Scott, but I do like him a whole, whole lot."

"I'll bet you do. He's kind and looks like a sex symbol on steroids. Does he have any available brothers?"

"Maybe I'll ask. I will see him later today."

"For more sex?" Lish asked, crunching on a piece of bacon.

"No! That is not all I think about with him. He's fun to be around."

"Mmhmm."

"He is!"

"I'm sure you're right. I'm likely projecting because horni-ness is taking over, and sex is all I can think about it. Don't mind me."

"I thought you had a guy on call to service those needs?"

"I did, but I fired him. He started falling in love, and I don't want that. At least not right now. I'm still healing from past relationship drama. I don't need to be polluting anyone else with my baggage."

"You're so wise."

"Get slapped around, and your heartbroken enough, and you'll wise up too. Finally, I am happy again. I like my life, and I love myself. No one is going to take my joy from me."

Piper raised her glass of juice.

"Cheers to that," she said.

Lish smiled and did the same.

The night was peaceful and calming. There were minimal cars out, and the temperature was perfect. Piper licked her strawberry and vanilla mixed ice cream cone, and Desmond took a scoop from his cup of cookies and cream. They were walking through downtown Atlanta enjoying the atmosphere and each other's company.

"I am getting my cable back next Sunday. Do you want to come over and watch some of my favorite shows with my best friend and me?"

Desmond lifted a brow.

"Come to your girl's night?"

"Hmm, I didn't think of it that way."

"How did you think of it?"

"A chance for you to meet my best friend and watch gory medical stuff on TV. You don't have to come, though."

"I never said I wasn't interested. If you want me there, I'm there."

"It's that simple?"

"It is."

Piper stopped and watched him lick the ice cream spoon.

She shivered, remembering when he used his tongue on her like that.

"What do you want from me, Des?"

"You mean right this second as I watch you eat that ice cream and fight hard, not to drag you back to the car and give you more orgasms than you can handle?"

"That wasn't what I meant, but now you have me intrigued."

His expression sobered, and he locked eyes with her, carefully touching her cheek.

"I want us not to stress anything. I think if we are friends first, it will make for a better relationship. You've dealt with a lot in the past, and I'm not here to add pressure. I only to make things better."

Piper offered him her hand. He took it, and they started walking again.

"That skill you have to get a girl wet on the spot is something otherworldly."

Desmond gave a sly grin. He knew what he was doing, but he meant every word.

"Speaking of otherworldly. What's up with Lacy and Vince?" he asked.

"Besides being the freakiest couple on the planet?"

"Okay, so I'm not crazy. I thought I heard a few insane things coming from their apartment, and not too long ago, I saw Vince in the hallway. He ran by me, and he was soaked. I thought it was sweat at first, but it smelled like piss."

Piper screamed with laughter.

"Sorry to be the bearer of bad news, Des, but that was pee. "

"Get the fuck out of here! You're kidding?"

"I'm not. I saw it with my own eyes."

"Damn, I get being freaky, but that's too far for me."

"You and me both. I think my wildest adventure was sex in public. What about you?"

"I've done the public thing before, and I used to have a sex swing."

Piper stopped. That comment sent her body into the heated zone rather quickly.

"That sounds hot. What happened to it?"

"I threw it out. I plan to get another when I buy a house."

Her mind whirled at the things he could do to her in a sex swing. Beyond the usual dildos and vibrators, Piper had never thought about gadgets like that before. Being strapped in while Des went to town on her pussy made her crave an outdoor treat that would be much sweeter than the ice cream.

Biting her lip, Piper asked, "Am I invited to play on your swing?"

"Do you even have to ask?"

"Just making sure I secured my spot."

Whatever Desmond was holding back was ready to be unleashed. Piper could see it in his eyes, and she felt her nipples get hard. He seemed to have a magnetic pull on her body, and she welcomed it to draw her in and let him have his way, however, whenever and wherever.

"Look over there?" he said.

Piper turned and saw a darkened narrowed pathway between two buildings that led to an office park.

"I don't see anything."

"Are you sure?"

"Yeah, it's just dark space for a short stretch, and then it opens out further down into a parking lot."

"Interesting," he commented, tossing his ice cream cup into a nearby trash can. "I see an opportunity."

"For?" Piper asked, interest piqued, but as soon as the word left her mouth, she understood his unstated suggestion.

They'd both had sex in public before but never with each other. In that small section before the lights pierced through the darkness, they could enjoy a moment of quick, hot intimacy.

Piper dropped her almost finished ice cream cone into the trash can next to his and decided to mess with him.

"I don't know, Des. I'm not even that turned on."

"I think you are."

"No. In fact, I don't want you at all right now."

"Piper, I am about five seconds from taking you right here on the sidewalk so everyone can see if you keep trying me."

"Oh, I dare you."

He picked her up and tossed her over his shoulder so fast, she gasped. Desmond then carried her into the darkened area, and once he'd pulled up her skirt and yanked her underwear off, he gave her every inch of the treat she'd been craving.

Two knocks on Piper's office door caused her to look up.

"Hi Piper," Julia said, a little hesitant. "You got a minute?"

"Yes, of course," Piper replied.

She stacked the papers she was working on and pushed them aside. Julia never came by her office, and the sudden appearance made Piper a little worried.

Julia entered the office and sat down in the small cushioned chair in front of Piper's desk. She was wearing yellow scrubs with ducks on them.

"Cute scrubs."

Julia looked down as if she'd forgotten what she was wearing.

"Yeah, on Monday's I work in the children's ward."

"That's sweet."

Julia took a deep breath before speaking, and Piper braced herself for something unsettling.

"I saw the billboard."

Piper winced internally.

"Oh, did it make you upset?"

"No, no, nothing like that. It's just . . . I'm driving to work, and bam! There's my husband larger than life being publicly broadcasted for cheating."

"You think we went too far?"

"Scott deserves everything that's coming to him. I'm getting my revenge; it's not fair that I block anyone else. Plus, it gave me more ammunition against him, so I thank you for that."

"Piper's brows furrowed.

"More ammunition?"

"The emails you forwarded to me. Or rather, your cousin did. Tina is her name, right?"

"Right."

"Either way, already four women have come forward for having had something to do with Scott. Two of them said they had a one-night stand with him. One said they dated for three months, and another is swearing she has a three-year-old by him."

"Wow. Do you believe them?"

"At this point, I can believe anything. Fortunately, it's the lawyer's job to get to the bottom of it. I've finally digested the enormity of the situation. I was married to a despicable man, and now all I want is to put my life back together. He's been pretending to work out of town so long that I realized I'm used to not seeing him, and any connection we shared ended a long time ago."

"That's understandable. Did you ask them about the life insurance thing?"

"I did, and taking out life insurance on your spouse is not illegal. However, it does require their signature, and I haven't signed anything."

"That's mighty ballsy of him."

"It's also yet another thing the lawyers need to sort through."

"Have you spoken to him?" Piper asked.

"Yeah, this morning. Can you believe that? He said nothing about you, the billboard, or any of it, and I didn't ask."

"That's weird. He knows that I know you exist. I'm shocked he didn't start apologizing to you on the spot. Especially after what I did to him in the park."

"What did you—" Julia stopped and raised her hand. "Nope. I said I don't want to know. I still mean it."

Julia shrugged and placed her hand on her forehead.

"Either way, who knows why he didn't say anything. Maybe he is avoiding it and trying to come up with an excuse. I didn't ask him any questions, so I guess he's not volunteering any information."

Julia looked at her watch, and Piper said gently, "I know I've asked you this before but are you sure you are okay?"

"Trust me, I am. I'm tired that's all."

"You still staying with your friend?"

"Yup. I'm not going back to my place with Scott. The lawyer actually said being separated is smart and makes things less messy. On a good note, they should be able to serve Scott with divorce papers in a little less than two weeks."

"That is good news."

Piper's phone vibrated on her desk, but she ignored it.

Julia stood.

"You can take that. I have to get back to my floor anyway."

She turned to leave and then stopped.

"Thanks, Piper. It's because of you that I'm going to be done with that asshole."

Piper offered a kind smile. She wasn't equipped for what to say in a situation like this.

Julia walked out of the office, and Piper glanced down at her still vibrating phone. It was Vanessa. Had to be. No one else called from unknown numbers.

"Hello," Piper snapped into the receiver.

She could be wrong about who the caller was, but she doubted it.

"Piper, you've been a bad girl," the woman said in a sing-song tone.

"Look at that, right on schedule. Every time I see Scott, you seem to pop up. What the fuck do you want, Vanessa?"

"I see someone has been doing their homework."

So, her name was Vanessa. The confirmation gave Piper a sense of relief and dread. Vanessa wasn't calling to say hello the bitch had something up her sleeve.

"Now that I have your name, finding you should be easier."

"You won't have to look far."

Piper was slow to ask the next question. Talking to Vanessa was always upsetting and strange, but today the eerie vibe was at an all-time high.

"Why is that?"

"Because I'll be seeing you real soon."

If Piper wanted to say something more, she didn't have the chance because Vanessa ended the call.

CHAPTER 8

J ake stared at her in confusion.

"But I don't get it. If it's your birthday, why do you have a surprise for me?"

Her cutesy and simple idea to tell Jake that the cable was getting turned back on hadn't made it very far.

A couple of minutes ago, Lish had called, and after Piper warned her normally uncensored best friend that virgin ears were listening, she turned on the speaker.

Lish suddenly started yelling "Happy Birthday" over and over again, and an excited Jake had joined in. It was indeed her birthday, and even though it wasn't a big deal to her, Lish always tried to make her feel special.

After Lish said goodbye, Jake flooded Piper with questions.

"How old are you? Where's your birthday hat? Are you having a party? Can we eat cake now?

"Jake, slow down. I'm 27, and there is no cake, party, or hat."

"But aren't you happy?"

"Of course, I am. I'm happy and grateful that God blessed me to be here at all."

Her mind wandered to her Aunt Delores like it had so many times that day. Aunt Delores always called her or sent cute cards every year on her birthday.

"Some people aren't able to be here," Piper said more to herself than to Jake.

"Well, if you are happy, why don't you celebrate? Who doesn't celebrate their birthday?" Jake asked with a soured face.

"Well, my mom wasn't always around on my birthday, so I grew up not doing anything. I guess I got used to it."

"Where was she?"

Piper thought of an appropriate lie.

"She was at work."

"On your birthday?" he asked with astonishment.

"Yeah."

"Every year?"

Maybe this wasn't such a good lie, Piper thought.

"Uh, yeah."

"That's sad."

"It's okay, Jake. Besides, I'm not sad about it. Plus, I have a surprise for you."

"But it's your birthday."

And that's where they were. Still stuck on a concept that Jake viewed as the world's biggest mystery. Why would she have a surprise for him on her birthday?

"Let's not worry about whose birthday it is. Do you want to hear about the surprise?"

"I guess so, but that's weird. Don't expect me to give you any surprises on my birthday."

Piper laughed.

"I won't."

Jake shrugged.

"So, what's the surprise?"

"Next week, when you return, you can watch cartoons again."

"Why can't I watch them now?"

"Because it won't be available until next week."

"Then that's not a surprise. A surprise is when someone shows you something and yells, surprise!"

"Think of it as a future surprise."

Jake stared at her like she had two heads.

This was pointless. Piper had been excited all week that her shows would be back in her life. Truthfully a portion of the excitement may have been linked to the fact that she would also be spending time with Lish and Des, but she ignored that part.

Jake wasn't impressed either way, so Piper thought of something else.

There was ice cream in the freezer, and deciding to abandon the topic altogether, she said, "Never mind, Jake. You want some ice cream?"

His eyes brightened.

"Because it's your birthday?"

Piper sighed.

"Sure."

"Yay!" Jake shouted, running to the kitchen.

Piper pulled a blue glass bowl from the cabinets and gave Jake two scoops. He sat at the kitchen table with two of his favorite toy race cars.

From the couch, Piper watched him take his first spoonful. He shoved it into his mouth messily, leaving traces of the chocolate ice cream on his lips, cheeks, and the tip of his nose. Before Piper could tell him to grab a napkin, he wiped his face with the back of his sleeve and dug in again.

Piper shook her head. She almost protested him using his

sleeve as a napkin, but the damage was done, and he looked so content.

Curling her feet underneath her body, she turned to stare out the window. There was a blue truck parked next to her car. She'd never seen the truck before, but that wasn't out of the ordinary because she rarely took inventory of vehicles in the parking lot.

The only reason she was doing so now could be summed up in one word, Vanessa. That psychopathic witch was up to something. On Monday, Vanessa had said that Piper would see her soon. What the hell did that mean? And could Piper do anything to avoid being caught off guard?

Keeping pepper spray close by and checking her surroundings were the only things she could think to do right now. Moving was not an option, and hiding was not her style.

So far, though, everything had been quiet. Vaguely, Piper wondered if Scott had anything to do with Vanessa's plan. Certainly, he was pissed; therefore, his participation in retaliation wouldn't be far-fetched.

Piper sighed and glanced at her purse. It was where her pepper spray resided. Maybe she should consider adding a gun to her limited supply of self-defense.

Regardless, Piper wasn't afraid.

If the bitch wants me, she thought. *She knows where to find me.*

Piper poured the entire bag of chips into the bowl and then did the same with another.

"Do you think this is enough?" Piper asked.

Lish added another coat of glittery red nail polish to her pointer finger and looked up.

"Piper, you have tons of food laid out. Stop stressing. Everything will be perfect. You were less nervous when I met Scott."

"That was because I didn't have a chance to be nervous. You stopped by out of nowhere to borrow makeup and shoes, chatted with him for 15 minutes, and then left."

"Was it really only 15 minutes?"

"Yeah. You said you were running late for work, and you guys only talked face to face that one time."

"I'm always late for work. I probably just didn't like his vibe."

"Ugh, don't remind me. Pointing out that you did distrust him reminds me that I didn't. You still haven't said, 'I told you so', by the way."

"I'm not going to."

"You sure? Giving you a chance here to do the best friend victory dance."

Lish pointed one glossy finger in the vicinity of her eyes.

"No, blinders, remember? Always easier to see crap when you're not in it."

"If that isn't the truth."

Piper took the bowls of chips to a living-room table, already filled with tons of snacks. She wanted to make sure that Des and Lish had an excellent time.

"When is Des going to be here?"

Piper glanced at the clock.

"In about 30 minutes."

"Good, that gives you time to calm your nerves."

"What?! I can't help it. It's not every day that my best friend meets my . . . well, boyfriend."

"I knew it!" Lish said, hitting the counter. Then she nervously checked her nails for damage.

"Hey, emphasis on friend."

"Whatever you say."

Lish resumed painting her nails, and Piper took a box of donuts to the living room. Once everything snack-wise was to her liking, Piper went into her bedroom and spent ten minutes freshening up. After covering her lips with yet another layer of cotton candy lipgloss, she heard a knock at the door. She rechecked the time. The cable guy should have been there already.

The company said he would arrive by 12 and that setup would only take 15 minutes, but the technician was a no-show. Hopefully, the person at the door was him and not Desmond. Piper wanted everything to already be in motion by the time he got there.

As she rounded the corner to open the front door, she spotted Lish lying on the couch with one foot in the air, wiggling her toes.

"What are you doing?"

I painted my toenails the same red color and wanted to get a good look at them. You know, like how people might view it from the audience?"

"I hope it passes your test."

Lish put her leg down and sat up on the couch.

"I think they're in for a sexy show."

Piper shook her head and opened the door. Des stood there holding a case of Sprite and a plastic bag with two bags of chips sticking out the top.

"Hi," Piper said, grinning hard.

Desmond always made her think of two things—happiness and sex.

"Hi."

He leaned down to kiss her on the lips before walking inside to place the items on the kitchen counter.

"You didn't have to bring anything. I invited you."

"I know, but I wanted to, and I remember you said Sprite is your favorite."

"It is. Thanks."

Lish got up from the couch and joined them.

"The last thing Piper needs is more chips," Lish said with a laugh, motioning to the table. "Hi, I'm Alisha."

"It's nice to meet you, Alisha. I'm Des."

"Oh, I know who you are. You're the guy that Piper can't stop thinking about."

Piper shot Lish a look that the girl ignored.

"That's news to me," Desmond said, pulling Piper close and giving her yet another steamy kiss.

"What have you two been up to today?" he asked.

"Mostly setting up snacks," Piper said.

"While I sample them," Lish added.

"Sounds good. Before I came here, I was watching college football."

Lish got excited, and Piper rolled her eyes.

"What's wrong?" he asked.

"That wasn't for you, Des," Lish said. "That was directed towards me. Piper hates how much I like football."

"I don't hate it . . . it's just . . . boring, and Lish can be over the top with her cheering."

"Hey, I only did that handstand one time! I told you it's only boring to you because you don't get it."

"And I don't want to. Medical dramas are more interesting than football."

"They're interesting, but not better than football. How about we watch a little today, and I will try, for the millionth time to explain it to you?"

Piper crossed her arms. The last time Lish tried to teach her about football, she got highly annoyed when Piper accidentally cheered for the wrong team.

"I promise I'll be good, and now you have a perfect reason

to learn," Lish said, winking at Piper and nodding her head in the direction of Desmond.

Piper looked at Desmond, and he put his hands up.

"Nope," he said.

"Nope, what?"

"Keep me out of the FFF."

"FFF?"

"Friends Fighting over Football."

Lish and Piper laughed.

"Even if I wanted to, I can't because the damn cable guy hasn't shown, which reminds me. I'm going to go call and find out what's going on. You two can talk about boring football while I'm gone."

"What team do you like?" Desmond asked Lish.

"Falcons all the way for me," Lish replied. "Even though they keep letting me down. I'm also good with The Saints."

"The Saints! We're already enemies. What Falcons fan likes the Saints?"

"I do! They're a good team!"

Piper picked up her cellphone and walked into the living room area, where she could hear better. Lish and Des were about to debate football teams, and Piper felt it was the perfect time to exit.

"It took 10 minutes to get someone on the telephone, but finally, a representative answered and informed Piper that there was a scheduling mix-up. The earliest they could have a technician out was tomorrow at 2 pm. Tomorrow was Monday. She would be at work.

"Do you have any appointments later in the day?"

"No, ma'am, after tomorrow, we don't have anything else until the end of the month. The only reason I was able to get you seen tomorrow was that someone recently canceled."

"Tomorrow is not good. Are you certain there is nothing else?"

"One second," the lady said.

Piper watched Desmond and Lish having their football conversation. She couldn't make out everything they were saying due to the God-awful hold music blasting in her ear, but Des was shaking his head, and Lish was highly animated, throwing her arms around.

It was easy to tell they were getting along. It made the outcome of not getting her cable installed today worth it.

"Ms. Fosters?"

"Yes," Piper said, putting all her attention back on the conversation.

"I looked to see what else I could do, but there isn't anything. Is there a possibility someone could let the technician in? As long as they are over the age of 18, it's fine if you aren't home."

"I can check. Hold on."

"Lish," Piper said.

Lish didn't hear her. She was mid-rant and pointing a finger at Desmond.

"I would know because I saw him in person, and he isn't that big. The man couldn't defend a marshmallow."

"Lish," Piper repeated, a little louder.

Lish stopped and faced Piper.

"What's up?"

"Are you available tomorrow at 2? It's the only time they can schedule my installation."

"Not tomorrow. I have more crap to help my sister with. I'm free Tuesday."

Piper shook her head.

"If it's not tomorrow, then it can't be scheduled until the end of the month."

Lish made a face.

"Yikes, that's a while. I'm sorry, sweetie. I know how bad you wanted your shows back."

"It's fine," Piper replied and readjusted the phone.

"I guess I'll have to accept your end-of-the-month appointment."

"Alright. Let me get you set up."

Piper sat down on the couch, a little disappointed but grateful to at least be seen before the month was over.

"I can do it," Desmond said. "I mean if you want me to. I don't have to meet my client until 4:30 tomorrow."

"Are you sure?"

"Yeah."

Piper quickly played the scenario over in her head. If she did this, Desmond would have to let the technician in, which meant he would need her key. Did she feel comfortable giving him a key to her place? Or being inside while she wasn't home?

After all this mess with Scott, she should be leery of trusting any man for a while. However, when it came to Desmond, she never doubted his honesty.

Into the phone, Piper said, "I'm sorry to be so back and forth, but I can take tomorrow's appointment."

"No problem at all. I'm glad you found someone."

Piper remained on the phone a few minutes longer to get everything set up and then went to join Lish and Desmond.

"Thanks again, Des. I'll give you my spare key so that you can get in."

"Okay. I'll drop it back off to you later tomorrow night. Also, since they aren't coming today, you want to watch your shows at my place?"

"We can do that, but instead of my shows, I guess I'll give football another try."

"Thank you, Des!" Lish exclaimed. "She's only doing this because of you, but I'll take it."

Piper slapped Lish's shoulder.

The three of them loaded up most of the snacks Piper had

set out and carried them to Desmond's apartment. As soon as they walked through the door, Dagger approached, trying desperately to see what was in their hands.

"Your food is over there," Desmond said, shooing Dagger towards his bowls.

Dagger looked to Piper and Lish. Lish avoided eye contact because she said she couldn't deal with the sad eyes.

"I'd give you some buddy, but Des is being mean," Piper said.

"I don't care. Blame me. Dagger will eat everything in our hands in under 30 seconds with no remorse."

"But he's so cute," Piper and Lish said, gushing over the dog.

"Have fun playing with him. I'm turning on some football."

That was all Lish needed to hear, and Piper reluctantly tagged along. All she knew was Lish better not start that "if you cheer for the wrong team, you're going to jinx the next play" crap.

However, Lish stayed on her best behavior, and 30 minutes into the game, Piper felt more comfortable, shouting and jumping with the other two fanatics.

Piper had to admit, watching football was fun. She still only understood the basics, and it didn't hold a candle to her medical dramas but watching it with two good friends made it more exciting.

Especially after Lish told Desmond what she did for a living, it opened up the floor for a trip down memory lane and hilarious stories Desmond refused to believe happened.

Such as the time, one of the club security guards, Trent, had to physically remove a customer standing in front of Lish's stage masturbating.

Trent was a big guy, and getting the disgusting customer out of the club should have been a piece of cake. The issue lay in the timing of the removal. A split second before Trent grabbed him, the guy ejaculated into his own hand, and once Trent tried to escort him out, the man fought back.

Trent ended up getting slapped in the face with a hand full of semen that covered his left eye and upper lip. Needless to say, Trent was so furious it took three other security staff members to pull him off the unlucky customer.

Then there was that time a customer named Gimp scared the shit out of Candi, one of the newer dancers, and caused her to fall off his lap and sprain her wrist.

Gimp was a retired war veteran that came to the club every time his wife put him out of the house, and because Gimp was a stubborn man who loved young women, he got put out a lot.

However, this time, knowing that his destination was the strip club, his wife decided to put him out minus one vital piece, his glass eye.

Candi wasn't aware of his war injury and became startled when she slid down seductively onto his lap and came face to face with a turned-on, one-eyed man, with slight traces of tobacco smelling drool dripping from his mouth.

All in all, the club wasn't known for dull moments, and Piper had many good memories from there. After the beautiful day she had with Desmond and Lish, more good memories were in the making.

CHAPTER 9

Bright and early Monday morning, Piper was out the door and fighting traffic to make it to work on time. Usually, being a few minutes late was no big deal, but today she had numerous meetings scheduled back-to-back that would keep her busy until lunchtime.

Piper entered the first meeting just as the director for her department, Jacob Mallory, was introducing himself. This meeting was for most of the staff in the building and was held inside a small auditorium-like room.

Piper waved to a few women she'd grown familiar with since working there and picked a seat in the back row to settle into. Next, the director began addressing proper protocols for the nurses, and Piper began to zone out. This portion of the conference had nothing to do with her.

She scanned the room in search of Julia. They weren't exactly friends, but Piper liked to know that the woman was doing okay. On the days Piper saw her, Julia always seemed so rundown. Piper found herself wondering, had Scott broken her? Put the last nail in the coffin, so to speak?

Julia already had so much on her plate with caring for

others and work. It wouldn't be unexpected if she simply collapsed from sheer exhaustion. Nevertheless, today would not be the day that she got to know if Julia was still standing because Julia wasn't in the meeting.

By lunchtime, which didn't occur until 1:30 because her last meeting ran late, Piper made her way to an almost empty lunch area. Management had purchased pizza for the staff, and Piper piled three slices onto her plate and went to find a table.

As she sat down, her cellphone vibrated in her pocket. It was Desmond.

"Hey you," Piper said.

"Hi. How's your day?"

"Long. So many boring meetings."

"Well, I have good news for you."

"I'd love some good news."

"The technician is here."

"Really? It's only," she checked her watch, "1:45."

"Yeah, he showed up early. I came over at 1:30 to ensure I didn't miss him, and I'm glad I did."

"That's wonderful. Des, you're a lifesaver. How can I ever repay you?"

"Tomorrow night, you can let me make you dinner while we watch one of those shows you are obsessed with."

"Deal. You still have work later today?" she asked.

"Yup. I should be done by 6:00, so I'll drop your key off no later than 6:30."

"It's fine. You can bring it to dinner tomorrow."

"You sure?"

"I'm positive," was all Piper said.

However, her naughty side fantasized about him using that key to enter her apartment in the middle of the night and give her something guaranteed to ensure sexy dreams.

They talked for another 15 minutes while the technician

worked his magic on resetting her cable. After a couple of tests to ensure everything was working correctly, he left, and Desmond and Piper said their goodbyes.

Two nurses entered the lunch area, chatting away.

Piper tried not to eavesdrop, but when she heard the nurse in the pink scrubs say, "This is her fourth time coming to the emergency room because the condom keeps getting lost all up in her business!" Her ears took on a mind of their own.

"The fourth time?" the nurse in the blue scrubs asked.

"Yes! I don't know how it keeps happening. I mean, are the guys starting the fun with the condom, noticing it's absent when the ride is over, and simply assuming that her vagina collects them?"

Piper couldn't help herself. That last part made her laugh out loud.

"Oh. I'm so sorry. I swear I wasn't trying to listen."

The girl in the pink waved her hand.

"It's fine. I'm sure you've heard crazier things working here."

"Actually, I haven't. I'm kind of new. My name is Piper."

"Hi, Piper. I'm Prisha," the girl in the blue said.

Prisha was short and adorable with a long brown braid that landed a few inches from her waist. She extended a hand, and Piper could easily make out her henna tattoos.

"I love your tattoos."

"Thanks."

"I'm Sanitra," the other girl said.

Sanitra was a few inches taller than Prisha and more striking in looks. She had short-cropped black hair, almond-kissed skin, and high cheekbones.

"Do you mind if we join you?" Sanitra asked.

"Please do. I would love some company."

The girls sat down and let even more hospital gossip spill.

Piper was on the edge of her seat during several stories and kept looking from Prisha to Sanitra as they divulged some of the juiciest details.

Lish was right. These two women officially made working at Juniper feel like living in one of the TV shows she loved.

Right before it was time to leave, Sanitra suddenly got very serious.

"Oh my goodness, did you hear about what happened to the nurse that works here?"

"No," Piper said, somehow not liking the distant and strange feeling developing in the pit of her stomach.

"She was in a terrible car accident. They had to rush her to the ICU."

"Yeah, I heard about that this morning," Prisha said. "I think her name is Julia."

Piper felt her heart stop and, in a shaky voice, asked, "Julia Bolden?"

"That's her," Prisha confirmed.

"I'm sorry, I have to go," Piper said, hurrying towards the elevator.

This "accident" had to be Scott's doing. There was no way this was some random coincidence. Piper had written off Julia dying in a car accident as another one of Scott's lies, when in fact, it was pre-planning. That lunatic intended to kill his wife. Or had he already killed her? Would Julia even make it?

Piper arrived at the ICU, panicked and uneasy. She made her way to the nurse's station, nervously tapping her pants.

The nurse took a few seconds to look up and then gave

Piper a warm smile. Her name tag read Patrice, and she looked to be in her early thirties.

"How may I help you?"

"Hi, I was hoping I could see Julia?"

"Are you family?"

Piper's shoulder's slumped.

"No. I only met her when I started working here."

"Oh," Patrice said in understanding. "Were you two close?"

"Sort of."

Piper didn't think it to be a total lie. They had dealt with the same man for a short period. Sharing the same dick had to buy you some level of closeness.

Patrice stared at Piper a moment longer and then said, "I know her too. Julia is a sweet woman. It's a shame that people can be so cruel sometimes."

"What happened?" Piper asked, not entirely sure she wanted the answer.

"You know that road about a mile from here with the small bridge? I think it's called Cambridge Drive."

"Yeah."

"Someone rear-ended her, causing her to lose control and drive over the edge. What's worse is they didn't even stick around to help or see if she was okay."

Piper's hand immediately flew to her mouth. This wasn't happening.

"I know it's so sad. The one saving grace is that her car didn't make it to the bottom because she slammed into a tree." Patrice seemed to consider her wording. "Of course, hitting the tree wasn't a good thing, but it quite possibly may have saved her life."

Piper lowered her hand and cautiously asked, "So she's going to be okay?"

"Only time will tell, but the doctors believe she has a really strong chance."

Hearing that made the knot in Piper's stomach loosen. Julia would be okay. Ryan would not lose his mother, and Scott would not get away with this. Maybe Julia saw something and will be able to testify against him. Patrice had already been pretty open about Julia's accident. Hopefully, she would remain as open with Piper's next question.

"Has anyone been to see her?"

Patrice gave her a quizzical look, clearly thinking the question odd. But Piper needed to know if Scott had been there, so she attempted to ease Patrice's suspicions by adding, "She told me she doesn't have much family, and I was hoping someone had been able to check on her."

The nurse's eyes softened.

"Oh, yeah. That's true. Only her friend that she listed as her emergency contact. We tried to contact her husband but haven't heard back yet."

Piper's nerves didn't know how to handle the fact that Scott was MIA. Did that confirm his guilt?

"Thank you for letting me know what happened. I'll be praying for her," Piper said.

"You can stop by again tomorrow if you'd like, and I can let you know how she's doing. I'm here from 6 am until 2pm."

Piper thanked Patrice again and rushed back to her office. She had to do two crucial things: call Lish and make sure her can of pepper spray was full.

"Are you sure you don't want me to come over?" Lish asked.

"You've called and asked me that three times since I told you about Julia. The answer is still the same. No."

Lish ignored Piper's rejection of her protective services.

"What about Des? You should at least call Des to see if he can come out and walk you inside."

"No, I didn't call him. He's at work."

"So! If you tell him why you're calling, maybe he will come home."

"I'm not going to do that. Besides, what is he supposed to do? Walk me to and from my car every day? Stop freaking out. I have my pepper spray, and I won't get out of the car without looking around."

"That's not good enough. I'm coming over there."

"You're too late because I'm already turning into the parking lot."

"Damn you, Piper!"

"Lish, I'm going to be fine. I'm sure my initial reaction made it out to be more than it was. Scott is a lot of things but not a killer."

Piper still wasn't so sure of that, but she didn't want Lish to worry.

"You're one stubborn broad Piper Fosters."

"That I am."

Lish blew out a breath and accepted her defeat.

"If something seems off, will you call me right away?"

"Yes. I promise."

Lish reluctantly ended the call, and Piper pulled into a parking spot.

As promised, she took a moment to look around before getting out of the car. She even placed her hand inside her purse for good measure to ensure that she could reach it quickly if need be.

Thankfully, the coast was clear. There weren't many cars

in the parking lot, and the only person outside was a lady talking on her cellphone.

Watching over her shoulder as she walked towards the building made Piper feel like an idiot. If this foreshadowed her new everyday routine, it was time to find a new place to live.

As Piper drew closer to the woman standing on the side of the building, it became easier to make out her conversation. She was short with a hazel brown complexion and reddish-brown hair cut into a slight bob.

"Lacy, I'm outside. I told you I'd be here on time. Just come downstairs."

A cigarette dangled from her mouth, and she was checking her pockets, possibly searching for a lighter. Suddenly the lady lowered the cell phone and covered it with her hand.

"Excuse me, you don't have a lighter, do you?"

Piper's first mistake was that she stopped. She should have kept moving or ignored the woman, but she didn't. She was almost at the door, and that had made her too comfortable.

Her second was removing her hand from inside her purse, choosing instead to adjust the strap on her shoulder before reaching for the door handle.

When an arm tightened around Piper's waist, and a thick metal object dug into her upper rib cage. She knew trouble had come.

"Hi, Piper. Did you miss me?" Scott said into her ear.

CHAPTER 10

The one thing Piper should be, she wasn't. There was no room to be scared. Pure hatred had consumed all her emotions. The woman standing in front of her was Vanessa; Piper was sure of it.

Scott was still behind her, pressing what she was certain was a gun into her side. Besides the annoying breathing in her ear, he was silent, probably expecting Piper to cry out for help or respond to his dumb-ass question about her missing him.

However, Piper's eyes were locked straight ahead, replaying all of the underhanded, demented shit this woman had done. The tires, the harassing phone calls, and that fucking, disgusting, bloody pad.

"Vanessa," Piper growled.

Vanessa tossed the cigarette into the bushes and dropped the phone she was pretending to talk on into her pocket.

"Aww, Piper, are you seriously upset? Didn't I warn you that Scott was mine? He used you like the whore that you are, and now he's going to get rid of you."

Then she stood on tiptoes and peered around at Scott.

"How did I do, baby? I could definitely be an actress, right?" Vanessa asked excitedly.

She was jumping up and down like some damn high school cheerleader, thrilled with the win.

Piper was going to put an end to that smile. Vanessa must have thought Scott could protect her; she was wrong.

Catching Scott off guard and Vanessa as well, Piper put all her weight forward and punched Vanessa in the face as hard as she could.

Vanessa went down like a sack of bricks, and before Scott could tighten his grip, Piper kicked Vanessa in the side. The girl rolled a few times, making grunting sounds that were akin to a wounded animal. Piper fought to get free. After everything Vanessa had done, she deserved so much worse.

"WHAT THE HELL?!" Vanessa shouted, hand touching her jaw and rage in her eyes. A trickle of blood oozed from the corner of her lower lip, and Piper could see the exact moment Vanessa realized she was bleeding.

"You bitch! You'll pay for that."

"Fuck you," Piper said and spat on her.

Vanessa was furious. She pushed herself off the ground and charged at Piper with a raised fist, and Piper continued to struggle to get loose.

"STOP IT!" Scott yelled.

Vanessa halted like a puppet on strings. On the other hand, Piper didn't give a shit about Scott's command until he pressed the barrel of the gun harder into her waist.

"Calm the fuck down, both of you."

"But that waste of space fucking spit on me," Vanessa whined.

"I don't care. We are in broad daylight, and I don't want anyone messing up my plans."

"But—" Vanessa started again.

"Not now," Scott warned.

Vanessa murmured like a child having a tantrum, and Piper smirked. Choking Vanessa out was still at the top of her list, but it felt good to see the girl upset, and it was a shame how much control Scott had over her.

Thinking of Scott shifted Piper's focus from Vanessa to the man holding a gun to her. Now that she'd released a little steam, terror started to creep in. She was in some real shit. Was he going to kill her?

"Hopefully, you two have gotten that out of your systems because I have some business with our girl Piper here."

He kissed her ear, and Piper cringed.

"What the fuck do you want, Scott?"

"Don't worry, you will see."

To Vanessa, he said, "I can take it from here."

"Are you sure? I can stick around?"

"We have to stay on schedule, Vanessa."

"I know but, we can move faster if it's both of us."

"I *said* I can handle it!" Scott yelled. Apparent irritation laced in his words.

Vanessa looked sad, and Piper felt like she was part of some sick game. What the hell was wrong with the girl? Letting Scott talk to her that way. Piper would have kicked him in the balls and left him in the street. Oh yeah, she had already done some version of that, which is why he was here pissed right now.

Scott seemed to realize the effect of his words on a cowering Vanessa, so he added, "You know I love you. Let's get this done so that we can move on with our lives."

That gave Vanessa the inspiration she needed. A broad smile took over her face, and everything in her seemed to brighten.

Yup, this bitch is crazy.

"I love you too. So much! Call me if you change your mind. I'll be at home waiting for you."

Scott said nothing. Instead, he grabbed a handful of Piper's hair and directed her towards the front door of the apartment building. The sudden pain caused Piper to gasp, but no other sound left her lips. She didn't want to give Scott the satisfaction of knowing he caused her any pain.

Piper concentrated all of her energy on figuring out a way to get out of this pathetic situation. She tried to adjust her hand and discreetly slide it into her purse.

"I wouldn't do that if I were you," Scott warned.

Piper's hand retreated, and she mentally cursed.

"Scott baby, did you hear me?" Vanessa called from a distance away.

Piper couldn't see exactly where Vanessa was behind them, but it couldn't have been too far.

"Yes. Vanessa. Fuck!"

"I just . . . I just . . . are you mad at me?"

Vanessa sounded like she was about to cry . . . again.

Scott took a deep breath.

"No, Vanessa, I'm not mad. I'll see you soon, okay? Love you."

"Love you too," Vanessa said, following up with kissing noises before she got into the car and started the engine.

Damn, she was fucking annoying. Piper wasn't ready for what Scott had planned next, but anything was better than listening to Vanessa's needy, whiny behavior.

"You sure know how to pick them," Piper said sarcastically.

"Walk," he commanded.

There wasn't enough time to think up a crafty idea to get out of this one. They made it to her front door quicker than she expected without running into any helpful residents.

For a split second, Piper had a sprinkle of hope when they passed Mr. Leo in the hallway, but Scott only pulled her closer to make his hateful hold on her seem like a loving embrace.

After opening the door, Scott shoved her inside, closing and locking the door behind them. Now that they were facing each other, Piper could take a good look at him, and she did not like what she saw. His eyes appeared wild, vacant, and, if she was truly honest, scary.

Whatever mask he had been wearing the whole time they were together was gone. He didn't even stand the same, and the ease with which he held that gun made her blood run cold.

"Put down your purse and kick it across the room."

She did so and instantly felt vulnerable. Her eyes quickly searched the room for weapons, and she mentally calculated the distance to the knives on her counter.

"I suggest you skip the stupid shit," Scott said, following her line of vision.

"I'm already pissed at you for leaving me in the fucking woods naked for the cops to pick up." His voice rose significantly towards the end of that statement, and he had to close his eyes to regain his composure.

Piper took a step back, and Scott's eye's popped open. He adjusted the gun so that it aimed at her head.

"Do not move another inch, or I'm going to put a bullet right in between your eyes." He rolled his shoulder and then added, "Fortunately for me, your ruthless deed helped me concoct a plan of my own."

Piper could only blink.

"Now, stay quiet and don't move. I have a call to make."

He pulled out a cellphone and gave her another threatening look filled with quiet rage.

"By the way, that was a nice touch creating that website exposing my secrets," he said, waving the gun at her.

"Scott, I—"

111

"Shut the fuck up. I don't want to hear from you right now."

Her temper rose with her panic, but she remained quiet and tried to discover a way to get out of this alive. The distance between them was too far, and he'd shoot her before she made it close at all.

Scott only pressed three buttons before hitting send and placing the phone to his ear. Once Piper understood that it was 9-1-1, her heart nearly quit on the job.

Was he calling to report a murder? My murder?

The operator answered, and Scott spoke in a hastened tone.

"My car has just been stolen."

"Yes, sir, Can you give me the car's description and license plate number if possible?"

Scott provided the answers to the questions, and Piper's brows knotted. She didn't see the car Vanessa left in since her back was to the parking lot, but a vehicle fitting that description was in the parking lot when she got home. Was that the car Vanessa and Scott came were driving? And if so, why had he just reported it stolen?

Scott finished up with the operator and shoved the phone back into his jacket pocket, giving Piper a devilish grin.

"I know what you're thinking. Why would he do that?"

Scott took a moment to study the gun and then looked up at a puzzled Piper, who was almost 10 feet away.

"Would you believe that I have been searching for a way to get rid of that annoying bitch for a while now? She's way too clingy for me. I swear I wanted to stab her sometimes."

He glanced away as if he'd suddenly realized that stabbing her was an option he had all along. Then he shook his head.

"Anyway, thank you for the idea with the cops. Now, Vanessa will be left holding the bag."

Piper couldn't resist.

"And how exactly will you do that? You just gave away your ride."

"Eh, I don't need it. My girlfriend will give me her car. Wait, I'm sorry," he said, putting up a hand. "Ex-girlfriend. I forgot we broke up. Hard to keep track."

Piper's eyes widened as her unfortunate outcome became crystal clear. If he planned to take her car, he had to know she would report it stolen, but Scott obviously wasn't worried about that because he was going to kill her.

Piper had to keep him talking and figure out a plan.

"But Vanessa loves you. You should keep her around."

Scott tilted his head.

"Are you stalling Piper?"

He said it as if he were reading her thoughts.

"I assumed you'd be ready to get this over with. But sure, I'll play along."

He crossed his arms and leaned back against the kitchen sink.

"It's true being the love interest to desperate, lonely women is a very profitable business. Too bad Vanessa is nuts."

"That's the pot calling the kettle black," Piper spat.

Scott pretended to be hurt.

"Now, why would you say that?"

"You used me, lied to me, and even tried to kill your own wife."

She was fishing with that last remark, but the way his face twisted into something sinister was confirmation enough.

"How could you do that to her? To Ryan?"

Scott waved the gun. His composure visibly slipping again.

"Don't you say his fucking name. That is my boy, and I'll raise him right. You have already done enough damage."

His eyes slowly traveled up and down her body. When he spoke again, he had regained his control.

"Sucks too. I had high hopes for you."

"What are you talking about?"

He smiled that evil smile again.

"Oh, Piper, you were perfect. A gorgeous, young stripper with mommy *and* daddy issues. It was like hitting the jackpot. I could smell the vulnerability of the lonely little girl inside you seeping off your skin. You wanted to love and be loved so bad; merely the promise of a future was all you needed."

Piper felt tears stinging her eyes as his words settled in because they rang true. She did love him, wanted to build a life with him, and trusted him.

"And let's not forget, the fact that you could stretch your legs from east to west in the bedroom didn't hurt. I really could have built my new life with you. I mean, that is until I no longer needed you, of course. But no, you had to play investigator, stick your nose in where it didn't belong, and ruin my years of hard work."

Piper tried to find the strength to remain calm, but it was a battle. The more talking he did, the more she felt her knees would give out, but his unfiltered confessions were also the only way she could buy more time.

That's when she remembered the woman at the fair that slapped him. The incident seemed like so long ago.

"The woman that day at the fair, she didn't make a mistake, did she? It was you who had the one-night stand with her and stole her grandmother's ring, wasn't it?"

"Oh yeah, what was her name again?" Scott said, snapping his fingers. "Nicole! That's right. She was fun for the moment. No one I'd spend more than a night with, way too annoying and needy as hell."

"What happened to your tattoo?"

He looked down at his arm as if the tattoo were still in place.

"Temporary ink is a cool invention, you should try it sometime. Oh wait, you can't because you will be dead. "

Piper swallowed.

"So you plan to kill me, now? Just like that?"

Scott slid the gun behind his back and pulled a small roll of tape and a black taser from his pocket.

"No, not just like that. I'm going to have a little fun first."

Piper looked horrified.

"Don't worry, I won't play too long. I do have a flight to catch."

Without warning, He rushed towards her, and Piper screamed. She ran to the living room, yanking up a glass lamp and throwing it at him. It bounced off his shoulder and crashed to the floor.

"Get the fuck away from me!" she shouted. She picked up a small glass statue from her living room table and threw it at him as well, but it missed and hit the wall.

He was no longer advancing towards her in a rush, which somehow made every step he took more measured and terrifying.

"You know what's surprising? I've never killed anyone before. You and Julia are my firsts. I had to kill her for the insurance money and you . . . well, killing you will be for fun."

Piper found another hard glass object to throw. This time it did make contact, but he barely seemed to notice. His eyes were fixed on her, filled with malicious intent and hatred. Julia and Piper may have been his first, but they would not be his last.

He was loving this, and Piper was growing more and more discouraged. She planned to lead him as far away from the front door as possible and try to run for it. It wasn't a great plan, but it was all she had.

Her cellphone was too deep in her purse, and running to her bedroom offered no protection because those doors may as well have been made of cardboard.

"Fuck you, Scott. You don't have to kill me, and you didn't have to hurt Julia. You have tons of money."

"Yes, but I'd like more."

Piper moved to the side, and Scott took two giant steps closer.

"This is fun. Watching the fear in your eyes multiply and knowing that I have all the control over what happens next. I didn't get to do this with Julia."

He was bragging and feeling cocky. He viewed her as nothing more than harmless prey in his demented game, and that got under her skin.

"Julia is going to live, you piece of shit. So, it looks like you failed after all."

Scott shrugged.

"As you said, I have tons of money, and I'll be gone long before anyone suspects me."

He suddenly stopped and retrieved the gun from his pocket.

"This has been fun, but I'm bored now. So get your fucking ass over here and sit down in that chair."

"What if I don't?"

She knew what would happen if she didn't, and it wouldn't be pretty, but even while staring death in the face, keeping her mouth shut felt impossible.

"I will shoot you in both legs and drag you over there. You see this?" he asked, pointing at the edge of the gun. "It's a silencer."

Her eyes traveled from the gun down to the floor, and that's when she saw it. A thick piece of glass from the lamp that had shattered. A few shards were near his feet, and it would be tricky grabbing one without him noticing, but if she could pull it off, it might save her life.

Piper reluctantly walked towards him. When she got close enough, he shoved her in the direction of the chair. The push wasn't hard enough to make her fall, but she did so anyway, pretending to stumble over her own feet as she concealed the glass with her body.

Scott rolled his eyes. "Get up, Piper, and stop being dramatic."

She used one hand to slowly push her way off of the floor and the other to secure the piece of glass. It was sharp and dug into her hand without mercy as she tightened her grip on it. She was probably bleeding, but an injured hand was preferred to being dead.

Piper groaned, "I think I hurt my ankle."

Out of her peripheral, she saw him lower the gun seconds before he grabbed hold of her neck and began pulling her to her feet.

As soon as he got her up onto one knee, Piper swiftly turned and sliced down the arm holding the gun.

Scott shouted a curse and dropped the weapon, but before she could land another blow, he backhanded her, and this time, her collision with the floor was not intentional. Pain exploded in her head, and for a split second, she couldn't hear or see.

"YOU STUPID WHORE!" He yelled, collapsing on top of her. The impact knocked the wind out of her, and immediately after that, Scott's hands were around her throat.

Piper dug her nails into his face, and Scott punched her several times before she withdrew. The excruciating jolts of pain raging their way through her body forced Piper to give up the fight a lot sooner than she wanted to. The ease in which he was overpowering and blocking her attempts at self-defense made Piper feel like an abused rag doll.

Scott squeezed tighter, and Piper felt her already restricted access to air become eliminated completely.

Deja Vu replayed in her mind. This had happened before. Scott choking her, the shortness of breath and intense levels of panic. That time it ended in smiles and cuddles, but this time it would end with Piper being united with her Aunt Delores.

Piper couldn't let that happen. She stopped trying to break his hold around her neck and dug her fingers into the deep cut she had made on his arm.

Scott cursed again, and his grip loosened immediately but not long enough for her to gain a sufficient amount of air. Her eyes were beginning to water, and her movements began to slow. Mentally she tried to push herself to move faster and kick harder, but her limbs felt too heavy.

She was dying, and vaguely two thoughts came to mind. Would Lish be okay? And she wished she could tell Desmond goodbye.

As if her thoughts conjured up the man, suddenly Piper's door swung open, and Desmond charged in. He tackled Scott, and the two men rolled a few times before Desmond got the upper hand and began punching Scott without pause.

Piper lay there coughing, the events around her moving too fast to keep up with. Her head was ringing, and she couldn't see out of one eye and just barely out of the other.

Sounds of glass breaking and furniture being collided with and knocked over seemed to come from all around her. Feeling around on the floor, she tried to concentrate. The gun had to be there somewhere. She was trying desperately to see, but only a sliver of light was making its way in.

She squinted and made out the black shape a few feet

away. Cautiously, Piper moved towards the gun but stopped abruptly and covered her head when she heard a loud crash.

The guys were grunting, cursing, and fighting so close to where she was, Piper braced herself, anticipating that at any moment, one of the punches Scott intended for Desmond or vice versa would land on her instead.

When nothing happened, Piper resumed crawling towards the gun, only to realize too late that it wasn't the gun at all but a black TV remote. Her curse turned into a horrified scream when a hand locked around her ankle and dragged her backward.

Piper blindly grasped for anything to anchor herself to. However, nothing could be found. When Scott flipped her over, she kicked as hard as she could, willing one of her strikes to land, but his iron grip wasn't loosening.

Just when she thought it was all over for her, a shot rang out.

"The next bullet takes your life with it," she heard Desmond say in an unrecognizable voice fueled with fury and hatred.

Scott released Piper.

"Hey, it's all only a misunderstanding," Scott said, obviously trying to talk an enraged Desmond down.

Not even two seconds later, Piper heard police rush inside shouting, "Drop the Gun, now!"

Piper's limited vision filled with blurs and shadows of movement happening all around her.

"Des! Des!" she called out.

"Everything's alright, Piper," she heard Desmond say."

He must have been across the room and unable to get to her. There was so much activity in progress it was difficult to pick any one thing to focus on.

Someone came over to her, but it wasn't Desmond. The

person helped her to her feet and introduced themselves as Officer Williams.

A blanket was placed around her, and officer Williams informed Piper that paramedics were on the way.

"Are you okay?" officer Williams asked.

Piper opened her mouth to speak but suddenly felt so tired and weak.

Was the room spinning?

The fragment of light coming in was now getting smaller and smaller. Piper felt her legs give way, and seconds later, the light was gone completely.

CHAPTER 11

I t was three weeks before Piper could return to work, and those were the longest three weeks of her life. Although she suffered no long-term damages, unless you count to her mental state, three weeks was how long it took for the bumps, bruises, and two black eyes to heal.

After the attack, Piper woke in the hospital, achy, confused, and upset. The constant rush of adrenaline coursing through her body had caused her to faint, and thankfully, Officer Williams caught her before she hit the floor.

The medical terminology for her reaction was called Vasovagal syncope. Piper remembered hearing it on one of her medical dramas and never assumed something like that could happen to her.

Then again, she also never thought she'd be running through her apartment trying to escape an ex-boyfriend that was set on torturing and killing her.

The worst part about trying to recover was that Piper could barely see for the first week and a half due to her swollen eyes. Nonetheless, once the facts of the horrific experience settled in, Piper figured maybe she was better off not seeing. It's not like her life was pretty right now; in fact, her entire world was upside down.

Her normally clean and classy apartment was a mess, from what Lish told her. The man she used to love had tried to kill her, and the man she was beginning to love had been arrested. Admittedly, she could see how cops bursting inside to see him aiming a gun at Scott would paint him as the bad guy.

Thankfully the charges against Desmond were dropped once everything was sorted out, but still, it was a rough start to a long three weeks.

Lish told Piper that she could stay at her place until she was better, but Piper declined. She felt more comfortable being at home, and it gave her a sense of control in an unruly situation. Plus, it's not like her bedroom was affected. The living room and part of the kitchen were the actual disaster zones.

However, being home may have offered Piper familiar surroundings, but she didn't draw much peace from it. Her apartment had become less like her home and more like a tourist attraction.

Friends, family, and acquaintances constantly stopped by to bring Piper cards, flowers, and well wishes. In addition to the people she knew, strangers were often dropping in. Maintenance specialists and cleanup crews came to fix damages to the apartment, and they made a lot of noise.

At first, Piper was surprised. To her recollection, she and Scott didn't ruin the place that much. All she remembered doing was dodging and screaming until Scott tried to choke the life out of her.

Then she learned it was when Desmond arrived on the scene that most of the significant damage occurred. Two angry men trying to murder one another had left her apartment in shambles. Holes were in the walls, the TV was broken, her coffee table was in pieces, and even a window had gotten knocked out.

Desmond was adamant about paying for any repairs and replacing her furniture, but Piper was simply grateful that he was there. If it weren't for him and Lish, Piper didn't know how she would survive this. It was a struggle waking up each morning and depending upon others for help.

Not to mention the continuous drop-by from police officers that loved asking her questions but barely answering any of hers. Piper didn't simply want to press charges; she wanted to know if they could handcuff Scott to the actual prison.

Per their request, Piper told them the story repeatedly about how Scott used Vanessa to catch her off-guard so that he could attack her. Then what transpired once they got inside the apartment, and finally what occurred once Desmond arrived or what she thinks happened since she could barely see.

Nevertheless, more questions of the same kept coming. Eventually, they moved on from Scott and started pressing her about Vanessa. Piper had nothing of substance to add. All she knew was that Vanessa was a psycho that Scott had been dating who spent months harassing her.

The cops still weren't satisfied with her responses, and ultimately, Piper pointed them to Jasmine for more answers.

Amongst all of the officers dropping by to question her, Officer Williams was in attendance several times. Piper kept waiting for the woman to ask as many questions as her fellow team members did, but for the most part, she only listened.

It wasn't until two weeks into Piper's recovery that Officer Williams visited Piper alone and filled in some gaps.

"How are you?" Officer Williams asked.

They were sitting in the living room on a new couch that Desmond had delivered the day before while Lish was making Piper something to eat.

"Pretty good. Since the swelling has gone down, I can see a lot better. The doctor said in a few more days to a week, I should be able to return to work."

"I'm happy to hear that."

The officer cleared her throat and placed the bottle of water Lish had given her on the table. She seemed nervous or maybe unsure of something.

"So what brings you here? Do you have more questions for me?" Piper asked.

The woman turned fully to face Piper. Her expression was serious, and her tone was straightforward.

"I'm not here on police business today. This is personal."

"Okay," Piper answered slowly.

"About eight years ago, I lost my youngest sister Maxine to domestic violence. There was a guy that she loved named Jeff, who wasn't worth loving. Maxine left him many times, but he always convinced her to return. The night he killed her was the worst night of my life. I had a feeling that I needed to go to her house, but I ignored it. I figured I would wait until my shift was over to do it. Needless to say, by the end of my shift, she was dead."

The woman paused, taking a moment to collect herself from a very raw and painful memory.

"I promised myself I wouldn't ignore that feeling again, and that's one of the reasons why I'm here today. You remind me of my sister, and you are the same age she was when she died. It seems that you have tried to make a good life for yourself, but I want you to know that Scott Bolden is bad news."

"Tell me about it. It took me a while to realize he was no good, but trust me. I get now."

"Any chance you're letting him back into your life?"

Piper laughed.

"Not a chance in hell."

The officer smiled at her. Piper could see the uncertainty in the officer's eyes, but Piper didn't take offense. After losing her sister and all the other similar stories, she'd probably encountered on the job. Skepticism was to be expected.

"Good. I also came here to give you some answers about Scott and Vanessa."

"Oh," Piper said, sitting up straighter.

"I'm sure I don't have to tell you that I could lose my badge over this, but as I said, I had a gut feeling about you."

"I won't say anything," Piper promised.

"Vanessa Langston met Scott about a year ago at Lancer Communications, where she worked. She said it was love at first sight, and he was the best guy she had ever met. He told her all the things you would expect. Such as he couldn't live without her, he wanted to marry her, and anything else that fits the dream guy package, and of course, she brought it. Technically, she's still buying it. Either way, a few months later, Vanessa says she found out that Scott was involved with you. But instead of being pissed, she asks him what does she need to do to convince him to choose her over you?"

"Wow."

"Exactly. Scott proceeds to tell her that he will end it with you after he gets back the money you owe him."

"What the hell?! I don't owe him anything."

"Yeah, we gathered that at the station, and we even told her that we think Scott was lying to her, but she won't listen."

"Wait. She *still* believes that Scott is a good guy in all of this?"

Officer Williams nodded.

"But he turned her into the cops. I was standing right there when he reported the car stolen to set her up."

"We told her that too, but she said it was you who must have called, and we are trying to turn her against Scott. The man that she loves." The officer rolled her eyes and added, "Those were her words, not mine."

"So he lies to her, gets her arrested, and she still refuses to see the light?"

"Refuses is an understatement. We found a black duffle bag inside of the car she was driving. I won't go into detail about the contents, but one of the interesting things we found was a car rental receipt with Vanessa's name on it. That car was later identified as the car that pushed Julia Bolden off the bridge."

Piper's mouth fell open.

"Vanessa tried to kill Julia? How did she even know about her? I thought Vanessa believed the same lie we all did about Julia being dead?"

"That's the thing. I don't believe Vanessa was driving that car, I think Scott was, and he's trying to pin it on her. But Vanessa's only response is that Scott wouldn't do that."

Vanessa was more controllable and desperate than Piper even thought possible. No wonder she would do anything to keep Scott to herself. The man literally could do no wrong in her eyes.

"Okay, well, with his back against the wall, did Scott finally confess to framing Vanessa?"

"Nope. When we asked him about it, he swears that Vanessa is some crazy stalker who wanted him all to herself and that's probably why she tried to kill Julia."

"How does he explain attacking me and her being with him?"

"He says that the only thing he is guilty of is having a big sexual appetite. In his version of the story, he came over here hoping to rekindle the flame with you. You agreed that you two could go up to your apartment and talk."

"Like hell I did."

"Hey, I wouldn't make this up. He swears that he looked out of the window during your conversation and "happened" to notice Vanessa approach his car with a black duffle bag, jump inside, and drive away. He called the police to report it, and you got angry and started hitting him after he confessed that he cheated on you with Vanessa."

"This can't be real," Piper said, adjusting in her seat. She was getting angry all over again. "And what does Scott say happens next?"

"That the guy you were cheating on him with bursts in and pulls a gun out on him."

"But it was Scott's gun and had his fingerprints!"

Officer Williams held up two fingers.

"We checked, and the gun isn't registered to him. Also, he claims his fingerprints got on there because at one point he wrestled it away from Desmond, but when you cut him with a piece of glass, he dropped the gun, and Desmond got the weapon back."

Piper's mouth fell open again. That bastard had made himself the victim and everyone else the villain. Piper had more questions and immediately started rattling them off. But for every question, Officer Williams provided a convenient answer.

"How did he explain Vanessa having keys to his car?"

"Says she must have made a copy."

"What about my bruises?"

"You fell during the altercation."

"On my face?!"

"That's what he said."

"He really does have an answer for everything,"

The officer put her hand on Piper's knee.

"It's all clearly nonsense, we get that, but he isn't confessing to anything. He sat there, cool, calm, and collected, either playing dumb or pinning it on Vanessa. He used her a lot, and if she doesn't give him up, we can't help her."

"I . . . I don't know what to say."

"I do. He's still going down. He wasn't a mastermind, just a smooth talker, and I have a hunch that he didn't cover all his bases. In the meantime, the assault charges from you and the possible involvement with his wife's attempted murder were enough for the judge to hold him and deny bail."

"I can't believe this," Piper said.

Officer Williams stood, and so did Piper.

"I'm sure I've said way more than I should, and we're still learning a lot, but I thought you deserved some answers."

"Thanks for that. It truly means more than you know."

Piper walked officer Williams to the door. The woman told her to take care of herself, and Piper promised she would before closing the door.

"Did you catch all that?" Piper said to Lish even before turning around.

"Every word! Lish replied, turning off the stove and ushering Piper back over to the couch.

"So Scott was playing, you, Julia, and Jasmine all while setting up crazy bitch? Shit, he is ruthless."

"He's a fucking maniac, and I hope he rots in jail."

"I'm with you on that. Listen, you need to get some more rest, and I'm going to finish making your lunch and straightening up. When Desmond gets here, I need to head out and do a few things before work."

Piper touched Lish's hand.

"What would I do without you?"

"For that first week, probably run into walls."

Piper laughed and pulled her friend in for a hug.

That evening Piper and Desmond were relaxing in front of the TV when someone knocked on the door.

"Ugh! Who is it now? It better not be another cop asking me stupid questions or some rando from the building wanting to get a look at my fading bruises."

"We can always ignore it," Desmond said.

"No. If I don't answer now. They are likely to return."

Desmond helped her stand and then collected their dishes from dinner off the coffee table and walked into the kitchen.

"Who is it?" Piper said.

"Lacy and Vince," Lacy shouted.

Piper and Desmond exchanged looks. Piper checked the peephole to confirm and then opened the door. Lacy was sporting a broad smile, and Vince was holding a beautiful bouquet.

Piper invited them inside.

"Hey, Des," Lacy said, giving Desmond a wave.

"Hey sweets," she said, turning to Piper. "We heard what happened with your ex. How are you holding up?"

Piper wasn't surprised. With all the activity and cops in and out of her place, she was sure the whole building had heard. Even Jake and Daya came over a few days ago to check on her and bring her a get well soon card. Her kitchen table was developing quite the collection.

"I've been better," Piper admitted.

"You've looked better too," Vince said, offering Piper the flowers.

She took them and placed them on the counter. She noticed Desmond pause while cleaning the dishes and she watched his jaw visibly tighten. She could practically read his thoughts. He wanted to pound Vince's face in for that comment. Lacy elbowed Vince, and he seemed confused as to what he said wrong.

"It's fine, Lacy. I know my face still looks a little beaten."

"That doesn't matter. It's not a nice thing for him to say. If he keeps it up, I'm going to have to pull out the ball gag."

Vince's eyes lit up.

"Don't threaten me with a good time, Lacy," he said.

Piper glanced at Desmond, but he simply shook his head and went back to washing dishes.

"Either way, sorry, we can't stay longer," Lacy said. "We only wanted to drop off these flowers and say we're glad you're okay."

"Yeah, cause for a minute there, I thought the police wouldn't get here in time," Vince added.

"You called the police?" she asked.

"Yup!" Vince said proudly. "I heard you scream, and immediately I knew something was wrong. I told the cops, 'get here quick. I just heard my neighbor scream, and it wasn't the good kind of scream where the dick makes you howl, but the bad kind like in the horror movies.' They said they'd be right over."

He was talking a mile a minute, and Piper was trying desperately not to laugh. When he finished, Piper gave him her sincerest thank you. He may have had a few screws loose, but he had helped to save her life.

"Thanks, Vince."

Vince smiled, and he and Lacy turned to go. Right before they stepped outside of the apartment, Piper remembered something.

"Lacy, do you know someone named Vanessa?"

Lacy considered the question.

"I can't say that I do. Who is she?"

Some girl Scott was involved with.

"I don't know, Vanessa, but I ran into Scott a few times in the hallway when you two were dating. He was always so kind and respectful. I still can't believe he tried to kill you."

"Me neither," Piper said.

Vince and Lacy left, and Desmond put his arm around her.

"Another mystery solved, huh?"

"Yeah. Now I know where Vanessa got the tip to pretend she was talking to Lacy. Scott gave her that name, knowing it would cause me to let my guard down."

"I should have killed him."

"If you did, you'd be in jail, and I would be alone."

"We can't have that now, can we?"

Piper shook her head, and Desmond kissed her gently before leading her back to the couch. She relaxed into his arms, and he pulled a blanket over them.

"Did you ever get your extra key back?" Desmond asked.

Piper had completely forgotten about that. It was the key she had given Desmond to let the cable guy in the day she got attacked. Desmond planned to return it to her after work that evening, but his client needed to reschedule, so he actually never went. He was tossing some trash into the garbage chute when he heard a scream coming from Piper's apartment. With the key still in his pocket, he decided to react first and ask questions later.

"Oh yeah, I did. It was with my things when I woke up at the hospital. I guess one of the officers must have seen it still in the door, locked up and dropped it in my bag. Thank God you had it. That was so scary."

She shivered as her mind replayed images that she desperately wanted to never think of again.

"Look at me, Piper," he said.

When she did, he cupped her face in one of his large hands and said, "No one is ever going to hurt you again, do you understand?"

Piper nodded.

"I love you, Desmond."

It had been on her mind for some time now. She was

hesitant to let her heart feel anything for anyone after the shit Scott had put her through, but the truth was, life was meant to live, and since Scott hadn't killed her, living is exactly what she would do.

His response was instant.

"I love you, too."

Desmond continued to stare into her eyes and carefully embrace her face. He was gliding his fingers over her bruises, and then he leaned forward and delicately kissed each one.

Once he made it to her lips, the gentle caresses transformed into an intense kiss that warmed Piper's body. In his arms, she felt secure, loved, and cherished. He wanted her, loved her, and even though she would have survived this on her own, it was easier and much more bearable with him.

Desmond followed her lead on whether or not she wanted to turn their sweet moment into a sexy evening. It was tempting, but honestly, she was enjoying this; lying in his arms, kissing, and forgetting the world.

A week later, Piper returned to work, and doing so, made her feel whole again. Not only had she missed this place, but it seemed she was missed as well.

Upon entering her office, she was greeted with countless 'Welcome back' balloons, banners, and cards, and she couldn't stop smiling.

After countless staff members stopped by to say hello, Piper got an additional piece of news that took her happiness to a whole new level. Julia had woken up five days ago and was doing so well she had been removed from ICU and placed in a regular room.

Piper decided to use her lunch break to visit Julia, but

before doing so, she went across the street to a yummy deli shop and grabbed two sandwiches. It felt rude to only get one, and Piper figured she would offer the second sandwich to Julia. If she didn't want it, Piper could always eat it for lunch tomorrow.

When Piper arrived in front of Julia's newly assigned room. The door was open, and Julia was in bed watching TV.

"Knock knock," Piper said.

"Piper! Hi."

Julia looked genuinely happy to see her. Piper thought the unannounced visit would be strange, but it was actually the opposite. Julia had survived something horrific, and so had she. Even though they were on different ends of a battle, it felt like they had somehow been in the war together.

"How are you, Julia?"

"I feel like I've been pushed off a cliff, but I'm still here," Julia said with a smile. "What about you? One of the nurses told me what happened."

Piper laughed to herself.

One of the main reasons she was excited to work there was due to the gossip she would hear about patients. Now that she was the talk of the office, she was reminded that gossip went both ways.

"I'm much better now. It took me three weeks to get here, and I still feel discomfort with certain movements."

"You and I should compare scars then."

"No need," Piper said. "Hands down, you've got me beat. How's Ryan?"

"He's great. My friend has been taking good care of him, and she's bringing him back tomorrow if you would like to see him."

"I would really like that."

Julia's eyes turned sincere.

"So what happened? You hear a lot of talk around here, but I'd rather hear it from you."

"I don't even know where to start, Piper said."

"You can start with Scott is evil, and he's going away for the rest of his life."

"Good starting point," Piper agreed.

They spent her lunch hour talking about work, Ryan, hobbies, and exchanged horror stories of their brush with death courtesy of Scott. When Piper pulled out two sandwiches from her bag and offered one to Julia, the woman was grateful to eat anything besides hospital food.

Piper returned the next couple of days on her break to visit Julia and spend a little time with Ryan. It was a great way to enjoy her first week back.

On Friday after work, Desmond took Piper out to a romantic dinner at a luxurious restaurant. He told her to dress to impress and had done the same on his end. He was wearing an expensive, navy blue three-piece suit that fit him so flawlessly he looked like he belonged on the menu.

After the waitress delivered their drinks, he passed Piper an envelope.

"What's this?"

"You tell me," he responded, waiting for her to open it.

Piper pulled out two plane tickets.

"Des, are you and I going to Hawaii?"

"Not quite."

Piper looked puzzled, and the excitement that was building took a pause.

"You, me, *and* my siblings are going to Hawaii."

Piper felt giddy.

"Are you serious? I get to meet Legs and the other Ash siblings?" Piper said.

"You do indeed, and Raquel," Desmond retracted. "I'm sorry, Legs, is just as excited to see you. She and all of my sisters have already included you in all their fun, girly activities."

Piper was touched. Not only did he want her to meet his family, but his family was also thrilled to meet her. She always wanted a big family, and being a part of Desmond's would be like a dream.

"I cannot wait to go! This is going to be so much fun."

Desmond's face couldn't have been more relieved. Maybe he thought she was going to say no. Or that the idea of time was his family was too much too fast, but on the contrary, it was perfect. She loved him and had no reason to fear getting close.

Piper took a moment to enjoy how deliciously sexy he was. The last time they were at a restaurant, they wanted one another so bad they couldn't even stay through the meal.

"You know what? On second thought, maybe I shouldn't go," Piper announced.

"Why do you say that?"

"Because the last time I was at the airport, the escalator tried to undress me."

Desmond chuckled, and then he leaned in towards her.

"Piper, if anyone is going to be ripping clothes off of you, it's going to be me."

They might make it through dinner, but it was most certainly going to be another early night.

"Well, in that case," she said, moving closer so that her lips were only inches from his, "When do we leave?"

THE END

If you enjoyed this book, it would mean the world to me if you did two things.

Leave me a review on Amazon and visit nickigracenovels.com to join my mailing list.

I have a lot more romantic, suspenseful, and thrilling books on the way, and I would love for you to be a part of the journey. Be blessed and always remember to read to escape and escape to read.

ALSO BY NICKI GRACE

Romance

The INEVITABLE ENCOUNTERS Series
Book 1: The Hero of my Love Scene
Book 2: The Love of my Past, Present
Book 3 : The Right to my Wrong

The LOVE IS Series
Book 1: Love is Sweet
Book 2: Love is Sour
Book 3: Love is Salty

Thrillers

The Splintered Doll
The Twisted Damsel

Self-Help

The TIPSY COUNSELOR Series
The Tipsy Dating Counselor (Summary)

ABOUT THE AUTHOR

Nicki Grace is a wife, mother, and author addicted to writing, spas, laughing, and sex jokes, but not exactly in that order.

Luckily for you, someone gave her internet access, and now you get to experience all the EXCITING, SHOCKING, and HOT ideas that reside in her head. She loves to have fun and lives for a good story. And we're guessing so do you!

Read more about her and check out more books at nickigracenovels.com

f facebook.com/nickigracenovels

⊙ instagram.com/nickigracenovels

Printed in Great Britain
by Amazon